# SARA

# SARA

## WHENEVER
## I HEAR YOUR NAME

### JACK WEYLAND

Deseret Book Company
Salt Lake City, Utah

First printing in paperbound edition, August 1992

**Library of Congress Cataloging-in-Publication Data**

Weyland, Jack, 1940–
    Sara, whenever I hear your name.

    Summary: a fifteen-year-old Mormon falls in love with a pregnant teenager who has moved into a foster home after being sexually abused by her stepfather.
    [1. Unmarried mothers—Fiction.   2. Mormons—Fiction.
3. Christian Life—Fiction]   I. Title.
PZ7.W538Sar  1987      [Fic]                          86-29071
ISBN 0-87579-070-4 (hardbound edition)
ISBN 0-87579-621-4 (paperbound edition)

Printed in the United States of America

10    9    8    7    6    5    4    3    2

# Chapter One

WHEN TRAVIS WAS FIFTEEN YEARS OLD, Sara came to live next door. Life has never been the same for him since then.

Ten years have passed since their first summer together, and yet even now she appears in his dreams and he sees her again the way she was then, in jeans and sneakers, her hair like scattered sunlight. In the morning after one of these dreams, he is haunted by her memory, and he wonders what it would be like to see her again, but of course he knows that is not possible now.

Gradually he has come to understand that what they shared was too fragile to survive in the adult world. And so, for him now, all that is left of Sara is his memories.

TRAVIS FITZGERALD was born and raised in Logan, Utah. His father, Dr. Howard Fitzgerald, was a professor of range management at Utah State University. The summer when Sara came, Travis's father was often out of town attending professional meetings. And even when he was not traveling, his duties as a member of a stake presidency kept him busy. Because of the many demands on his time, he found it necessary to delegate responsibility; that summer he had assigned to Travis care of the yard and garden.

Each morning when Travis awoke, he found a list of

assignments on the kitchen table, left there by his father, who always woke at five o'clock, left for work at six, and returned twelve hours later. Supper was served at six fifteen. His father's meetings began at seven and often lasted past ten.

Ruth, Travis's mother, married when she was eighteen, in her first year at USU. She met her future husband, then a tall, lanky, quiet-spoken returned missionary, at a college dance. Five months later they were married. Travis was the last of their five children. They had raised four other sons, who had by that summer all left home.

During those hectic years, Ruth always had in mind to someday finish college. She had even taken an occasional course. Lately, however, she had become aware of the rapid passage of time in her life. Whatever she was going to do, she decided, she'd better do it soon. That summer she enrolled as a full-time student.

For Travis, there were advantages to being the caboose of the family. His older brothers had gradually worn down his parents, so that by the time he reached his teens, they gave in easily, allowing him more freedom than any of his brothers had experienced at the same age. But Travis was also Howard and Ruth's most conscientious son, and they trusted him. They hoped that with him, they might possibly escape the turmoil they had experienced in getting their other four boys through their teenage years.

And then Sara came.

TRAVIS STILL REMEMBERS the day Sara came. It was an afternoon in early June. He was mowing the front lawn and had just stopped to refill the gas tank when a car with State of Utah insignia on the side pulled up in the

Townsends' driveway next door. A woman wearing glasses that made her look like a friendly owl opened the door and said to her passenger, "Well, this is it. Let's go in."

A girl, almost as tall as he, with long blond hair, stepped out of the car. Although Travis suspected she might be good-looking, at that moment she looked either scared or sick, he couldn't tell which.

"Don't worry," the woman reassured, "everything's going to be okay."

The girl nodded, but with little enthusiasm.

"We'd better get your things," the woman said. From the trunk of the car they retrieved a tattered old suitcase with a rope tied around to keep it from coming undone, and a cardboard box heavy with books. The two of them, the woman short and plump, the girl tall and willowy, made an odd combination as they struggled to the door with their loads. The woman rang the doorbell, and Joan Townsend opened the door.

Travis had always liked Sister Townsend. In their ward she served as a member of the activities committee, and so she was always busy with one project or another. She was the only adult woman he knew who could do a cartwheel. On a dare she'd proved it at the last ward picnic, along with a playful challenge to any other mother to match it. Nobody had.

Joan was married to Gary, a salesman for an office-equipment company. He was more practical and down-to-earth than his wife. Together they seemed to make a good combination.

"Sara, this is Mrs. Townsend," the woman said.

"Hello, Mrs. Townsend," the girl replied.

"Hey, just call me Joan. Come in and I'll show you to your room." They went inside and closed the door.

Travis reached down and started up the mower.

THE NEXT AFTERNOON, as Travis went in the backyard to trim the hedge, he discovered the girl next door asleep in a recliner lounge parked in the shade of a tree. A book lay in her lap, its pages fluttering in the gentle breeze.

He stopped in his tracks. The girl was beautiful. He felt as if she were a shrine dedicated to beauty and that he'd come as a pilgrim from a distant land to pay homage. He stood there, awestruck, and stared at her.

After a while, he felt guilty about invading her privacy. He decided he'd better start working. With a loud snap of the shears he took a bite of the hedge.

The noise startled the girl. She gasped and sat up quickly, panic in her eyes, looking around, trying to get her bearings. Finally she found the source of the noise. She glared at him. "Go away."

"How come you're so jumpy?"

"I don't like people sneaking up on me."

"I wasn't doing anything wrong." He realized he was blushing. "My dad told me to trim the hedge today. That's the only reason I'm here."

Her expression softened a little. "Sorry. What's your name?"

"Travis Fitzgerald. What's yours?"

"Sara Corwin."

"Why are you staying with the Townsends? And why did you come in a state car?"

She looked away. "I just did, that's all."

"Where are you from?"

"I was born in Colorado, but we moved to Ogden a couple of years ago."

"Are you a Mormon?" he asked.

"No. Are you?"

"Yeah."

"How old are you?" she asked.

"Fifteen. And you?"

She paused. "Almost sixteen."

"Almost sixteen? That means you're fifteen then too, right?"

"So?"

He smiled. "What's the matter? Afraid to admit you're the same age as me? When's your birthday?"

"July ninth," she answered.

"Mine's September eighteenth." He paused. "We're only two months apart. So you're a little older." He smiled. "But two months probably hasn't aged you that much over me, right?"

He meant it as a joke, but she didn't take it that way. She looked sad, almost melancholy. "Sometimes I feel like a hundred years old."

He was confused by her sudden change of mood. "Are you going to be here all summer?" he asked.

"Yes." She picked up her book and stood, about to go inside.

"Maybe we could do something while you're here," he blurted out, surprising himself for being so bold.

"That's not a good idea." She started toward the house.

"Why?" he called after her.

"It's too hard to explain," she said, still continuing on her way.

"I'd like to be your friend while you're here."

As she turned to face him, her expression was one of despair. "And what would we do, go out on dates?" She sounded as if she were trying to torment herself.

"It won't be a date. We'll just do something together—go swimming or something like that. Anything you want."

"You're friendly now, but in a few weeks you won't even talk to me."

"That's not true."

"Yes it is." She continued toward the house.

He called out after her. "How about if we just go on a hike together? Give me a chance, Sara. You'll need at least one friend while you're here, won't you?"

She stopped, turned around, and slowly came back. At the hedge, across from him, she picked off a leaf and shredded it one section at a time, as if doing that would help with the decision. "I'll ask Joan what she thinks. If it's okay with her, then I'll go on a hike with you."


JOAN SAID SHE THOUGHT going on a hike with Travis was a good idea, and so the next day Travis let Sara borrow his next oldest brother's ten-speed bike, which had been stored in the garage for a long time.

They rode up to the mouth of the canyon to where his favorite trail began. When they started, he went first, but because he kept getting too far ahead of her, he let her take the lead. There were advantages in that because he could watch her. He liked how the breeze caught her hair. She was the most beautiful girl he'd ever seen.

Because the day before she had seemed so set against anything even faintly resembling a date, he decided to treat her the way his brothers had treated him when they first took him hiking. When they reached the place where the trail started, as he was taking things out of the bicycle carrier, he said, "There's just one other thing."

"What?"

"Out on the trail you're not a girl to me."

She looked at him strangely.

He couldn't help but turn it into a joke. "You're a moose."

She smiled but not as much as he thought she should have.

"Seriously, what I mean is I'm not going to baby you. It's the way my brothers taught me about hiking. You're on your own. I'm not going to treat you like a girl. Okay?"

"Good. I don't want to be treated like a girl."

He handed her a daypack and a poncho.

She looked at the poncho. "What's this for?"

"In case it rains."

She glanced up at the sky. "It's not going to rain." She gave it all back to him.

He took the items back and returned them to the bicycle carrier, then packed one poncho in his daypack, as well as a plastic bag of trail mix, a canteen, and a sack lunch he'd made for them.

They started up the trail. "This is easy," she said at the beginning. But soon the trail got steeper. After a few minutes of hard climbing, they sat down to rest. He gave her some trail mix to munch on. When they started off again, she kept the trail mix, which meant, because she kept falling behind, that he didn't have anything to eat.

The next time they stopped, he retrieved the trail mix back from her. Then he noticed what she'd done. "You ate all the M&M's from the trail mix?"

"Yeah. I don't like granola or peanuts—I just like chocolate."

He sifted through the mix with his hand. Sure enough, there were no M&M's.

"Is something wrong?" she asked.

"It's just that you're supposed to pull out a handful and eat it, and not go sorting through it just to get the M&M's."

"I'm sorry. I didn't know."

"There's certain rules of the trail, and one of them is you don't eat all the M&M's from the trail mix."

"I said I was sorry, didn't I?"

"I wouldn't have mentioned it except we agreed I wouldn't treat you like a girl." He paused. "But that's hard to do."

"Why?"

"Because of the way you look. You're beautiful."

She shook her head. "Don't say that." She seemed tense and nervous. "I shouldn't have come up here with you."

"Why not?"

"Because I've got enough problems already. Can we go back now?"

He shrugged his shoulders. "Sure, it figures. Girls always give up before they reach the top."

"Is that so?" she demanded, glaring at him.

"Yeah, that's so."

"We'll see about that." She started jogging up the trail.

The race was on. He deliberately paced himself. After a few minutes, he passed her. He hiked until he was far ahead of her and then sat down to rest. While he waited, he looked up and noticed dark clouds moving toward them. He heard thunder a few miles away.

A few minutes later she came straggling up the trail. She'd removed her sweatshirt and tied the sleeves around her waist. When she got to where he was sitting, she sat down to rest. Her forehead was covered with sweat, and she was struggling for breath.

It started to rain. He pulled out the poncho from the daypack and put it on. "Don't look at me like that," he said. "I had a poncho for you back when we started but you said you didn't want to carry it. You had your chance, so that's it. The one who carries the poncho is the one who gets to use it when it rains."

"Travis, I'm not supposed to get wet. The doctor told me to take care of myself."

He paused. His brothers had never given in to him,

but that didn't matter anymore. "All right, come here and we'll share."

She shook her head. "I don't want to sit that close to you."

"Why not? I won't bite."

She wouldn't budge.

"At least get under a tree." She didn't move. He couldn't stand to see her get wet, so he took the poncho off and handed it to her. "Here, go ahead and use it."

"How will you stay dry?"

"Don't worry. I know how to take care of myself."

Gratefully she slipped into the poncho.

He stood under a tree and marveled at how strange it was that a girl could get him to give up his poncho in a rainstorm.

"Travis?" she called out a short time later.

"What?"

"I guess it's okay if you come over and we share."

He draped the poncho on a branch above her, then sat down beside her. They were both leaning up against the same tree, their shoulders touching. He could smell the shampoo she'd used that morning.

"I bet you even like it out here in the rain, don't you," she said.

"Yeah, sure." He grinned. "It's because I feel at one with nature." He imitated a TV announcer. "Yes, out in the Bora Bora jungle, kayaking down the Pundgy-Manga River, eating maggots and raw crocodile, we all felt at one with nature."

They started laughing. It was a delicious experience. He knew he'd never forget this moment because of the smell of the pine trees and the rain and because they had laughed together and because their shoulders were touching and because her hair had brushed across his cheek and because she was the most beautiful girl he'd ever known.

"I'm sorry for being so mean," he said. "I've never had a girl for a friend before. I guess I don't know how to treat one." He smiled at her. "But, hey, I'm willing to learn."

Her expression clouded over. "Don't like me too much."

"Why not?"

She didn't want to talk about it. "Do you know any games we can play while we're waiting for the rain to stop?"

"When you were a kid, did you ever play paper, rock, and scissors?"

"No."

He held up two fingers at an angle. "Okay, this is scissors."

At least he got her to smile again.

He made a fist. "And this is a rock." Next he held his palm down, fingers together. "And this is paper. Okay, here's the game. Scissors cuts paper. Paper covers rock. Rock breaks scissors. We go, one, two, three. Like this. At three you make one of those three signs. Okay, one, two, three."

They played the game until it stopped raining.

"We'd better go home now," she said, standing up.

"Let's climb all the way to the top."

"I'm tired. You go. I'll stay here."

"Okay, see you around." He started up the trail. "Oh, by the way, if a bear comes along while I'm gone, don't panic. Bears can sense panic."

It was inevitable. "What does a bear do when it senses panic?" she called out.

"It goes in for the kill." He started up the trail again, pleased at his little joke, knowing it was only a matter of time.

"You're not fooling me!" she shouted. "I know you're lying."

"Maybe, but are you willing to risk your life on it?"

"Travis, tell me the truth, are there really bears up here?"

"You ever hear of Bear Lake? Three guesses why they call it that, and the first two don't count."

"Wait up."

They walked together side by side up the trail. Because he knew she was tired, he let her set the pace.

"Is it very much farther?" she asked a few minutes later.

"Not much."

She wiped her brow. "This better be worth it, that's all I can say."

"Once you get on top, you can see tomorrow coming." He paused. "That's what my dad says when we go hunting."

"Do you like your dad?"

"Yeah, he's okay."

"You're lucky. I wish my stepdad were dead."

He glanced at her. He could tell she was serious. He wondered why she was so bitter.

Finally they reached the top. They sat down, and he pulled out a couple of sandwiches and gave her one.

"It's been about a hundred years since I had a peanut butter and jelly sandwich," she said, removing the sandwich from its plastic bag.

"We were out of bologna. I made it myself." He took a bite and slumped over, pretending to die from food poisoning.

She smiled.

They had a wonderful time eating and talking. Her natural mood seemed to be one of sadness, but if he happened to say something really funny, he could get her to smile. It was spectacular to watch—it was like during a dreary, rainy day when a sudden break in the clouds appears and for a brief instant the sun shines through. He tried his best to keep her happy, to keep away the sadness that lurked somewhere in the corners of her mind.

He was fascinated with her eyes, not only because of their beauty, but because they reflected so accurately the way she was feeling. When he saw the sadness returning, he tried even harder to make her happy again.

At one point she became aware of how closely he was watching her. "What's wrong?" she asked.

"Nothing, I just like to look at you."

She frowned. "I wish you wouldn't say things like that."

"Why not?"

"It makes me nervous."

"Why?"

"It just does." To change the subject, she asked him to point out places they could see from where they were.

"Over there's USU, and that building there is the hospital, and there's the mall. We can almost see our houses but the trees are in the way."

"What's that building?" she asked.

"That's the Logan Temple. It's one of our church buildings."

"What's it used for?"

"They do weddings there."

"It looks like a nice place to get married."

"It's not just because of that. If you get married in the temple, you can be married forever, even after you're dead."

"Does everybody in your church get married in the temple?"

"No. You have to be living right before they'll let you in."

She stopped talking and finished her sandwich. The sadness in her eyes had returned. "We'd better start down," she said.

On the way down, no matter how slowly he went, she kept getting further and further behind. Finally he walked back up the trail to her. "Are you okay?" he asked.

"I don't feel very good. Can we stop a minute?"

"Sure." They sat down.

A few minutes later, she said, "I think I'm going to throw up. Can you move away? I don't want you to see me."

"I'll leave the canteen here for you," he said, setting it down next to her. He walked a small ways away. A minute later he heard her gagging. She was on her knees, bent over, throwing up. Afterwards he heard her rinsing her mouth out. And then it sounded like she was crying.

"Are you okay?" he called out.

"Yes," she said weakly. She stood up and came down the trail toward him. Her face was chalky white.

"Do you want some help?"

"No. I just need to rest for a while." She sat down and closed her eyes. "I hate the way I am."

"What do you mean?"

She opened her eyes and looked at him. "Nothing." She struggled to her feet. "I'm ready to go now."

They started walking again. "Is there anything I can do?" he asked.

"No. I'm better now."

But a short time later, she had to stop again. "I'm sorry."

"No problem."

She sat cross-legged on the ground, her back against a large boulder. He saw where the sun was and worried that if they didn't hurry they'd still be on the trail after dark.

She read his mind. "Go ahead without me if you want. I know how to get home."

"I'd never leave you here all alone."

"You'll miss your supper."

"I don't care."

"I'm sorry for being such a bother."

"Hey, it's okay. Besides, it was probably the sandwiches."

"No, they were fine."

Just to have something to talk about, he asked how long she would be staying with the Townsends.

"At least until January."

"Don't worry about the first day of school. I'll help you with everything."

"I'm not going to high school this year." Her voice was weak, her head down, her shoulders slumped over.

"Why not?"

"I'm just not, that's all."

"School's not so bad."

"I know. I like school, but I'm still not going."

"You can't just decide you don't want to go to school. There's laws that say you have to go. I know it's tough to start at a school where you don't know anybody, but I'll make sure you meet all my friends. You'll be a sophomore too, won't you?"

She nodded.

"Okay then. We might even have some classes together. So don't worry, okay? Everything's going to be all right. Oh sure, the first couple of days might be tough, but hey, it'll be hard for me too because it's my first year in high school, but we'll get used to it. You know what, I bet you'll end up liking it better here than where you came from."

"Please stop talking about school," she said.

He couldn't understand what he'd said to make her feel so bad. "I was just trying to be helpful."

She sighed. "I know."

"Why won't you tell me what's bothering you?"

"I can't."

"If you tell me, then I'll be able to help."

"Nobody can help me now."

"Sara, please, I want to be your friend."

She started crying. He didn't know what to do. He wanted to comfort her, but he didn't know how. He had no experience in that. Nobody had ever needed him before. Feeling awkward and clumsy and uncertain, he began to pat her on the shoulder the way his mother had done to him when he was little. He could sense the presence of her muscles and her collarbone. He thought it amazing that someone as beautiful as she would have such ordinary things as bones and muscles.

His hand momentarily rested on the fabric of her cotton T-shirt. He imagined that at one time it had just been an ordinary T-shirt in a store, but when she bought it, it gained special status among shirts because it had the honor of being worn by her. He realized that his sensations and feelings and thoughts were getting all jumbled up.

She reached up and gently placed her hand over his, which was still resting on her shoulder. To him it meant he'd comforted her. It made him feel good to know that.

"Sara, tell me what's bothering you."

"I can't."

"Why not?"

"It's too awful."

"I'll understand."

"No you won't."

"Why won't you trust me?"

"Please don't ask me any more questions." She forced herself to stand up. "We'd better start back now."

They walked slowly down the trail. "I'm sorry for messing up our hike," she said softly.

"You didn't mess anything up. When we were eating lunch together, it was the best time I'd ever had. You're the nicest girl I've ever known."

"Stop it, will you! You don't know a thing about me."

"Tell me then."

She sighed. "Oh, what's the use? You'll know soon enough. Maybe it's better if you hear it first from me."

"What?"

She hesitated and then, speaking so softly he could hardly hear her, she began. "I'm pregnant. That's why I came to live with the Townsends. They're my foster parents. The state arranged it all."

"You can't be pregnant," he stammered. "Not you, Sara . . . because . . . you're not like that."

"It was my stepdad that got me pregnant."

He didn't understand. "Your stepdad?"

They sat down.

"Yes. His name is Dillon Brenner. He married my mom when I was ten. When I was eleven, he told me he was going to teach me some things. At first it was touching, but it kept getting worse, and he just kept at it, more each time. I tried to tell him no, but he was my stepfather, and I was only eleven, and I thought I was supposed to obey him. He told me if I ever told, I'd be in big trouble. He just kept it up, for five years. Two months ago he got me pregnant."

"Why didn't you make him stop?"

"You don't say no to daddy." The bitterness in her voice scared him. "When he got drunk, he was a different person. Sometimes he hit me when I wouldn't do what he wanted me to do. He said if I ever told anyone, he'd kill me. It was awful. It was like the worst nightmare you've ever had, except that it would never end. It went on and on, week after week. Nobody can know how bad it is unless they've gone through it. Getting pregnant wasn't so bad. At least it meant they had to get me away from him."

There was a long silence. They could hear the birds singing in the trees. It sounded out of place with what they were trying to deal with.

"Aren't you going to say anything?" she asked.

He couldn't look at her anymore. "I don't know what to say."

"At least tell me what you're thinking."

"Your own stepfather?"

"Yes."

"He started when you were eleven years old?"

"Yes."

He felt sick. "Things like that aren't supposed to happen."

"I know, but they do. I'm not the first one it's happened to."

"When it started, why didn't you tell somebody what he was doing to you?"

"I told my mother, but she wouldn't believe me. She said I was making it all up. But later she told me that if it was true, then it was my fault for leading Dillon on."

"Leading him on?" Travis said. "You were eleven years old and he was a grown man. How could she say that to you? Why didn't she believe you?"

"I think she knew that if it was true, and she pressed it, it'd end up with her divorcing Dillon. She'd already had one divorce, and she was afraid of getting another one. It wasn't much of a marriage, but it was better than nothing. Sometimes when they'd been drinking, if they got into a fight, she'd yell at him to go get his little tramp, meaning me. So maybe she believed me but couldn't face it sober."

Because he didn't know what else to say, he stammered, "Do you want your baby to be a boy or a girl?"

She sighed. "I don't care. I just want to have it and get it over with. I'm going to give it to the state. They'll put it up for adoption."

"And then what will you do?"

"I don't know, but one thing for sure, I'll never go back home again."

"I don't blame you."

"You won't ever want to see me again, will you," she said.

He took a long time before responding. It was hard for him to understand what it had been like for her. He realized things would never be the same. But even so, she needed a friend. "I still want to keep seeing you," he finally said.

"Your parents might not want you to be with me when they find out."

"Why?"

"Some people'll think I'm a bad person because I'm pregnant and not married."

"It wasn't your fault. You just got a rotten deal, that's all."

She started sobbing. He put his arm around her. She rested her head on his shoulder. He could feel her tears getting his shirt damp. More than anything he wanted to be someone she could trust. A long time passed without any words between them. They heard the birds celebrating the end of the day with a song. That place became their refuge from the storm.

And then she moved away from him. "It's getting late, isn't it? We'd better go home. I'm feeling better now. Thanks, Travis."

They started down the trail. He stopped often to let her rest.

By the time they arrived home, it was nine o'clock.

His parents were gone, but they'd left a note on the table telling him to heat up the plate of food in the refrigerator. The note also reminded him to practice the piano because he had a lesson Thursday.

It seemed strange to Travis that he'd ever thought a piano lesson was important. He felt as if he'd aged ten years since breakfast.

# Chapter Two

THAT NIGHT SARA COULDN'T SLEEP. Each time a car drove by, she imagined it was Dillon out looking for her. She feared he'd kill her if he ever found where she was staying.

At two o'clock in the morning, she got out of bed and tiptoed down the hall. She passed Joan and Gary's bedroom. Because it was a warm night, they'd left their bedroom door open. She could see the two of them sleeping, husband and wife, comfortable and easy with each other, with everything natural and right. As they slept, they looked like little kids and not foster parents. Gary's glasses were carefully laid on the small table next to their bed. Without them, he couldn't see anything.

Gary was losing his hair. Sometimes Joan kidded him about it. That night he'd read to her about a new cure for baldness. Joan said she couldn't possibly love him more than she already did, hair or no hair. And besides, they needed the money to get the car fixed.

Sara entered the bathroom. She turned on the light and looked at herself in the mirror. She didn't look pregnant yet. She dreaded the day when she'd have to start wearing maternity clothes. She glanced around the bathroom. It was so strange to be living in this home, not even with relatives, just someone the state had assigned, purposely chosen far away from home because of her fear of Dillon.

Sara glanced at the bathroom scales. Joan was on a lifelong diet that never quite worked. Every morning she weighed herself. On the days she lost, she proudly announced it to the world. On the days she gained, she didn't say anything about it.

Sara went in the kitchen and looked in the refrigerator for something to eat, but nothing appealed to her. Finally she poured a glass of milk and sat at the kitchen table in the dark. Outside she could hear crickets. It was a nice sound. She sat in the dark and waited for the night to end. She wondered if she'd ever be able to sleep through an entire night.

Sometimes lately she played a game. She'd close her eyes and pretend she was shrinking, getting smaller and smaller until she was just a dot. Sometimes she wished she could vanish into empty space.

There was a butcher knife on the table from when Gary had cut a watermelon. She picked it up and gently rubbed its blade lightly over her wrist, not hard enough to cut. It would be easy to put an end to all her problems. But she wasn't a quitter, at least not yet. She remembered a teacher who used to say, "Quitters never win, and winners never quit." She wondered if that teacher would ever know how important that had been to her.

She heard someone coming. She set the knife back down on the table.

Joan turned the light on. "Sara, are you okay?"

"I'm fine. I couldn't sleep, so I decided to have a glass of milk."

Joan sat down. "Want to talk?"

"That's all right, I'm okay. You go back to bed."

Joan saw the knife next to Sara and picked it up and put it in the sink. "Anytime you want to talk, just let me know. Even if I'm asleep. Okay?"

"Okay."

"You've got your whole life ahead of you."

"I know."

Because Joan was only ten years older, it was hard for Sara to think of her as a foster mother. She seemed more like an older sister.

"Hey, I've got a great idea," Joan piped up. "Why don't we bake ourselves a cake?"

"Now? It's two o'clock in the morning."

"Good. That means we can eat it without having a bunch of kids begging. I've got a cake mix in the cupboard. Why don't you start on it while I shut the bedroom door so we don't wake up Gary."

When Joan returned, Sara was mixing the cake by hand so the noise wouldn't wake anybody up.

"You haven't said much about your hike with Travis," Joan said, getting two eggs from the refrigerator.

Sara paused. "I told him all about me."

Joan looked over at Sara. "Oh. What did he say?"

"He said he still wants to be my friend."

"Good. What do you think of him?"

"When I was crying, he put his arms around me and I didn't mind. I mean, I wasn't scared. His touch is like having a butterfly land on you—you hardly know it's there. I'm usually so jumpy, you know, but somehow I knew that Travis'd never hurt me."

"Yeah, Travis is a great guy. I like to have him baby-sit my kids because he makes up games and reads stories. He doesn't just sit around watching TV like some do. We like Travis a lot. How about you?"

Sara hesitated, not knowing if she should even say it. "Yes, I like him."

"He's kind of good-looking too, isn't he."

"It's not his looks I like most."

"What then?"

"I don't know how to explain it—it's like his goodness shines through." Sara stopped. "That sounds really dumb, doesn't it?"

"Not at all. I know what you're saying. That's what attracted me to Gary."

"Joan, you like being married, don't you?"

"Are you kidding? I love it. It's my whole life."

Sara hesitated and then decided to say it. "I worry that I'll never be able to get married now, you know, and be a wife."

"You mean because of what Dillon did to you?"

"Yes."

"Most men aren't like Dillon."

"Maybe I shouldn't ask this, and you don't have to answer if you don't want to, but is Gary gentle with you?"

"Yes. He's very gentle and considerate."

Sara nodded. "I thought he would be. Is it okay that I asked?"

"Sure, it's okay."

"I'm afraid when I get old enough to get married, no guy will want me after he finds out what happened to me."

"If he really loves you, it won't stop him. Sometimes a husband has to be patient while his wife sorts things out."

Soon the cake was in the oven, and they sat at the table. "I'm so glad you told the caseworker you'd let me stay here," Sara said.

Joan smiled. "Hey, think of all the free baby-sitting I'm going to get out of you. Gary and I'll probably take a long vacation and let you stay here and take care of the kids. Good luck with the little darlings. We'll send you a postcard once a week."

"You're not fooling me. You wouldn't get ten miles away before you'd be on the phone, asking how they are."

"You've really got me pegged, don't you."

Sara picked up an orange from a fruit dish and slowly began to rotate it. "The state attorney's office wants to know if I'll agree to testify against Dillon. What do you think I should tell them?"

"It's a hard decision, isn't it?"

"If I agree to testify, then I'll have to go back to Ogden and face Dillon and my mother. I'm not sure I can do that."

Joan nodded. "That'd be a hard thing to do, all right."

"But if I don't, then he'll get off scot-free. He ought to pay for what he did to me." She paused. "Sometimes I wonder what Dillon's doing these days without me."

"What do you mean?"

"I wonder if he's trying to find another girl to take my place. I couldn't stand to know that someone else was about to go through what happened to me. It makes me want to stop him." She set the orange down. "But sometimes, like tonight, I get so scared of what he'll do to me if I testify against him. At night, when I hear a car drive by, I think it's him. He used to beat me when I wouldn't go along with what he wanted. One time he started hitting me on the back with a golf club. I thought he was going to kill me. I still have scars from it. Sometimes I get so scared, it's even hard to breathe."

"You poor kid—you've been through a lot. Look, just wake me up when you're having a bad night."

"I hate to be a bother."

"You're no bother." Joan got a big grin on her face. "Besides, who else can I get to bake cakes with me in the middle of the night?"

"You're fun to be with." Then Sara sighed. "There's something else I've been worrying about—what will it be like talking to the psychologist?"

"If you want, I'll sit in with you the first time."

"No, I'd better do it myself."

A few minutes later the timer dinged and they took the cake out. Instead of waiting for it to cool, they had it right away with a glass of milk. By the time they finished, there was only one piece left.

"Well, I feel good now," Joan said. "How about you?"

"I'm not afraid anymore."

"Terrific," Joan said. She picked up the one remaining piece of cake and studied it. "You know, it seems a shame to leave such a small piece for an entire family. I mean, they're just going to get in a big fight about who gets it. Whataya say we finish it off? Then nobody'll fuss about not getting any."

They both started giggling like little kids about to do something naughty. They ate the last piece, then washed up so nobody would be any the wiser in the morning. Joan even opened some windows so the odor would be gone by morning.

"Let's do this again sometime," Joan teased. "Of course, we may both end up looking like the Goodyear Blimp. But at least you'll have an excuse. Actually, if you think about it, it's not that bad because we didn't put frosting on it, so it's not that many calories. Well, okay, it's not as good for my diet as an apple maybe, but on the other hand, who on earth'd ever get up in the middle of the night to eat an apple? Well, anyway, it was fun, and I'm glad we did it."

"Me too. I guess I'd better get some sleep or I'll fall asleep for the psychologist. Good night."

"Wait a minute," Joan called out.

"What?"

"I've got a complaint. How come Travis gets a hug but I don't? I mean, after all, I ought to get one once in a while too, shouldn't I?"

Joan opened her arms wide and hugged Sara. "You

and me, kid. Together we'll make it through whatever happens. Is it a deal?"

"It's a deal."

They said good night and Sara went to her room and crawled into bed and went peacefully to sleep.

# Chapter Three

SARA WASN'T THE ONLY ONE who couldn't sleep that night. A few blocks away, Kathy Briggs lay in bed and thought about Travis.

She had liked him for as long as she could remember, even as far back as grade school. But Travis had little use for girls back then. When she and Travis were both thirteen, she finally confided in her mother that she liked Travis but he didn't seem very interested in her, or any girl, for that matter.

"In some ways a boy is like an apple tree," her mother had said.

"Oh, Mom," Kathy grumbled, certain that her mother couldn't possibly know anything of value about the subject of boys.

"It's true. You've had enough experience with that old tree of ours in the back. You might want apples in July, but even though they look like apples, they have to mature. You have to wait until they're ripe. In some ways, Travis is like that. He's got his own clock that'll tell him when it's the right time for him to get interested in girls. Girls usually get to that stage before boys do. Just be patient—Travis's time will come."

And so Kathy became the impatient gardener waiting for Travis to ripen. She wondered what happened to a boy to change him from someone totally uninterested in girls to a guy who'd hang around a girl's house for as

27

long as you'd let him, which is what her older sister's
boyfriend had done before they got married.

Kathy told all the girls her age in the ward that Travis
was hers. They seemed to respect her claim. And so, the
way she figured, it was just a matter of time.

The older she got, the more Kathy grew to cherish
Travis's features—his brown hair and green eyes. He
was going to be a handsome man, and yet, oddly enough,
that didn't seem important to him. Through the years,
she had collected her favorite Travis memories. They
were like precious jewels in her mind. Sometimes at
night, just before falling to sleep, she took them out one
by one.

ONE OF KATHY'S MEMORIES OF TRAVIS was the first
time she danced with him. It was at their first youth conference. At the beginning of the dance, she'd noticed
him standing along the sidelines. Then their bishop
walked up to him and said something. Suddenly Travis
went into action. He moved through the crowd, his eyes
darting from one group of girls to another. Finally he
walked up to a girl and tapped her on the shoulder and
asked her to dance. The girl shrugged her shoulders and
went out on the dance floor with Travis.

After the music stopped, Travis began the search all
over again. Sometimes, like a shark closing in on a tuna,
he nervously circled the same group of girls several times
before going in for the shoulder tap.

Kathy realized that if she stayed alone and not a part
of a group of girls, it'd be easier for Travis. Keeping one
eye on his position, she moved so as to be in his path as he
made a sweep of the crowd.

It worked. He came up to her. "Want to dance?"

They began dancing. "The bishop challenged me to
dance with ten different girls tonight," he said.

"Oh."

"You're number four."

"Oh," she said again, not knowing what else to say.

"It's ten o'clock now," he said. "If I can do one every fifteen minutes, I figure I can go over my goal."

"If you ever run out of new girls, I'll dance with you again."

"The bishop said it had to be ten different girls."

"Oh," she said, disappointed in their bishop.

Travis never came back that night for a second dance with her. But on the way out of the building after the dance, he saw her. "I got my goal," he said proudly.

"Good," she said glumly. She was discouraged until she realized that maybe this meant Travis was getting interested in girls. That cheered her up.

ANOTHER TRAVIS MEMORY happened after a youth service project. A small group was still at church, and Travis was in the gym shooting baskets with some friends.

Kathy saw Travis's shoes on the floor. As a joke she hid them. After Travis's game, he began looking for them. Someone told him they'd seen Kathy take them.

He came up to her. "All right, what did you do with my shoes?"

"Your shoes? Did you lose your shoes?"

"C'mon, I know you took 'em."

She giggled. "I don't have your shoes. See?" She showed him her hands.

"Where did you hide 'em?"

"Why don't you look?" she teased.

"Okay, but you've got to come with me and tell me if I'm getting warm or not."

He held her arm, but not very hard. She could have broken away if she'd wanted to, but she didn't want to.

"Cold, cold, cold," she said as they entered the chapel.

When they approached the kitchen, she chanted, "Warm, warm, warm . . . hot . . . very hot . . . burning hot." There in the empty garbage can lay his shoes. He retrieved them and sat down to put them on.

"Here, let me tie them for you," she said. She knelt down and tied his shoes. It felt strangely wonderful to be doing something like that for him. She realized she was blushing.

"I never knew you were such a tease," he said.

She looked at him. "I am—with the right person."

He smiled at her. "Well, you'd better watch out, that's all I can say, because someday I might hide your shoes too."

"I wouldn't mind, as long as you help me get them back."

Just then Travis's mother came to the gym and called for him. He said goodbye and left.


KATHY'S NEXT MEMORY OF TRAVIS took place at a church sledding party. Travis had the biggest sled. Most of the time he'd go down the steep snow-blanketed hill with other guys, but one time, he asked her if she'd go with him. She said yes, and he held the sled while she sat down on the sled. He sat down behind her, put his arms around her waist, and pushed off.

On the way down, all she could think about was the fact that Travis had his arms around her. Near the end of the ride they were going so fast they spilled. Both of them rolled down the hill before coming to a stop.

"Are you all right?" he asked, hurrying over to her.

She sat up. "I'm okay."

"I'm sorry we wiped out. It's that turn. It's always

tough to get past it without turning over." He extended his hand and pulled her out of the snow. "Here, let me brush you off," he said.

He brushed the snow from her jacket. Suddenly she wasn't cold anymore. She thought winter was the best time of the whole year. She could have taken off her jacket and not even have been cold. She wanted to go down the hill again and again with Travis.

They did go down one more time, but then Melissa Bradbury had the nerve to ask Travis to take her down one time. And Travis, always the nice guy, said yes. Kathy stood on the top of the hill and jealously watched them go down the hill. Much to her delight, they made it all the way to the bottom without spilling, which meant that Travis didn't have to brush the snow off Melissa's jacket.


KATHY STILL COULDN'T SLEEP. She got up and went in the bathroom for a glass of water. She scowled at her reflection in the mirror. She didn't like the way she looked. She had reddish brown hair, blue eyes, and, especially in the summer, freckles. Most of the time she felt betrayed by her face and body and would have gladly traded them with nearly any other girl in school. Her features seemed so plain and ordinary to her.

She had been wearing glasses since fourth grade, but she was working hard to convince her parents to let her get contact lenses. Sometimes she went to the mirror and took off her glasses to see how she'd look with contacts. But without glasses, she couldn't see well enough to find out. All her friends told her she'd look good with contacts, so she kept pressuring her parents and saving the money she earned baby-sitting. Someday soon she'd get some.

She was pretty sure Travis would like her better with contacts, but, then again, he might not even notice.

She couldn't believe how unobservant boys were. The question she always asked in front of the mirror was, What would Travis like? She would have done anything to find the answer to that question. But it was impossible to find out, because when she asked Travis, he'd say he liked everything.

One time she asked him, "Do you like my hair this way?"

"Yeah, sure."

"Do you like it better this way than the way I used to have it?"

"Gee, I guess I don't remember how you used to have it."

Boys, she thought. Who needs them?

She knew that if her mother were aware she was standing in front of a mirror so late at night, thinking of ways to make herself more appealing to Travis, she'd scold her.

Kathy went to her room and lay down in bed. She looked at her clock. It was two in the morning. Time to sleep. Just one more memory. Last winter she had asked Travis to come over so they could study for a test. After they'd studied for a long time, they'd gone into the kitchen and made popcorn, and afterwards they'd sat next to each other and watched TV. There was a hairbrush nearby. She picked it up and started brushing his hair. He didn't seem to mind, and so she brushed it into silly styles and then got a mirror and showed him, and they laughed together. Sometimes as she styled it, she ran her fingers through his hair. It felt very nice.

Someday, she thought, he'll become as interested in me as I am in him. Someday he'll notice me as more than just a study partner. Someday he'll think I'm pretty.

Someday he'll ask me out on a date. Someday he'll ask me to go with him. Someday he'll kiss me good night. Someday he'll ask me to write him on his mission. Someday he'll come home from his mission and we'll get married in the temple.

Someday . . . someday . . . someday . . .

She fell asleep.

# Chapter Four

THE NEXT MORNING, while Travis weeded the garden, Sara came to the hedge. "Hi," she said, uncertain as to how he would treat her.

"Hi."

"Did you tell your parents about me?" she asked.

"No."

"Why not?"

"They got in too late."

"Are you going to?"

"I suppose so, if they ask."

"Are they here now?"

"No."

"Can I come over?"

"Sure, if you don't mind watching me work."

"I don't mind." She came over and sat on a lawn chair near where he was weeding.

"Are you sore today?" he asked.

"No, I think the exercise was good for me." She paused. "Except I couldn't sleep last night. Joan woke up and we made ourselves a cake and ate it all by ourselves, but don't tell any of her kids. After that I went right to sleep. I woke up just about half an hour ago. Joan let me sleep in."

She watched him work and then, out of the blue, said, "Can I talk to you about something?"

"Sure."

"The state wants to make Dillon stand trial, but first they have to make sure I'll testify against him. Sometimes I get scared. He said he'd get me if I ever told on him."

"He can't hurt you if he's in jail. Besides, I don't think a man should be able to do what Dillon did to you and walk away without some kind of punishment."

She slowly nodded. "That's what I was thinking too. I guess I'll go ahead with it."

"Do you want to go in and have some lemonade?"

"I guess so."

He opened the screen door and let her in. "My mom's not home. She's on campus, so don't complain if the service isn't very fancy."

"I won't."

In the kitchen he got out a pitcher of lemonade from the refrigerator, two glasses, and a package of Oreo cookies, and set them down on the table. "How do you eat an Oreo?" he asked.

"The normal way. Why?"

"I open each half, cut out the frosting, and just eat the cookie part. So if you like the frosting, you can have all of mine."

"No, after the cake last night I'd better not."

"Do you want to see the rest of the house?" he asked after they ate their snack.

"Sure."

In the living room she stopped in front of some pictures of his brothers. He told her a little about each one. Then they sat down at the piano and he played one of the songs he'd written.

"That was good," she said.

"Someday I'll write a song for you."

"I'd like that."

Next he showed her his father's office. One wall contained nothing but bookshelves. A computer and a printer were on the desk.

"What does your dad do?" she asked, taking one of the books from the bookshelf.

"He teaches at the university."

"What does he teach?"

"Range management."

"What's range management?"

He grinned. "How to manage a range."

She laughed. "You're full of useful information, aren't you?"

"Sure." He paused. "He's written some kind of a computer program. It's called CATTLE-1."

"What does it do?" she asked.

He smiled. "It goes out and rounds up the cattle."

"Oh sure."

He loved to see her smile. He wanted to run ahead and sweep away the obstacles in her life.

They wandered outside. She sat down on the back steps. As he started to sit down beside her, he put his hand on her shoulder the way good friends do.

"I'm going to get as big as a house," she said, to warn him of what was coming.

"I know. My brothers' wives are pregnant all the time. And at church there's always a bunch of pregnant women. So it's not like I've never seen it before."

"I'll probably end up barely able to get through a doorway."

"If you do, you do. It's no big deal."

"It's a rotten way to start a friendship though, isn't it?"

"Maybe we'll end up better friends than we would have otherwise. Tell me some more about yourself."

"Have I told you about my dog Muffin?"

"No."

"I got him when he was just a puppy. He's a miniature poodle. He's the cutest dog in the world, and he's smart too. He can do tricks like sit up and roll over. Whenever I come home from school, he comes out to meet me, all excited, wagging his tail and running around. He used to know when I was feeling bad, and he'd come over and lick my face and sit down and put his head on my lap and I'd pet him, and then everything'd be okay again. I asked if I could bring him here with me, but my caseworker said it wouldn't work out. But after I got here, Joan said she wouldn't have minded as long as he stayed outdoors because dogs make Gary sneeze. Travis, if there's some way to get Muffin here, will you help me build a doghouse for him?"

"Sure, I'll help you."

"Thanks. You know, since I've been staying with Joan and Gary and their kids, we pray a lot. It's the first time I've ever had family prayer. They're always saying they're grateful for this and grateful for that. At first I couldn't think of anything to be grateful for, but now I do. I'm grateful for Joan most of all, but also, Travis, I'm grateful for you." She reached over and placed her hand on his arm.

Travis felt elated. Just then Joan called out for Sara to come help her.


WITH SARA GONE, Travis went back to work. One of the jobs on his dad's list was to dust the tomatoes with insecticide. He went in the garage and grabbed the red tube of tomato dust, then went to the garden and began pumping out the white powder that killed tomato mites. He made each tomato bush look as if it had just snowed.

He was just finishing when he noticed a state car pull into the Townsends' driveway. Two men in short sleeve shirts and ties went to the door. He could hear the doorbell ring.

He went to the kitchen to look at his father's job list. Along with the list there were two ten-dollar bills and five singles with a small note that told him not to forget to pay his tithing and to put money in his missionary fund. He put the money in his jeans pocket and went back to the garden to thin out the carrots. As he pulled out every third carrot plant, he kept glancing over next door. The car was still there. He wanted to know what they were talking about. He could hardly wait for Sara to come and tell him.

He worked in the garden for an hour, then went inside and practiced the piano. After going through his lesson material, he worked on a song for Sara. Not much came of his attempts. After a while he quit and made himself a bologna sandwich.

While he was eating lunch, the phone rang. It was Alan Benson, a friend of his.

"Want to go swimming?" Alan asked.

"I guess so."

"How'll we get there?" Alan asked.

"I don't know. My mom's gone. Can your mom take us?"

Alan went to talk to his mother, then came back on the line. "My mom says we ought to ride our bikes."

Travis wished he were old enough to drive and had his own car.

He glanced out the window and saw the state car driving away. He decided he wanted to talk to Sara more than he wanted to go swimming with Alan. "I guess not, Alan. Maybe tomorrow."

He went outside and puttered around the garden so it would be easy for Sara to come out and talk to him. But she didn't come. A while later he saw her leave with Joan in a car.

He felt bad about not being able to see Sara. He went inside and phoned Alan, but Alan's mother said he'd already left to go swimming.

Travis rode his ten-speed to the swimming pool and found Alan. The pool was too full of little kids to get much swimming done, so they went to the deep end and did cannon balls off the low diving board, trying to see who could make the biggest splash. Alan, who weighed twenty pounds more than Travis, usually won.

Kathy was there too. She was lying on the cement drying off. He went over and sat down by her. "Hi, Kathy."

She smiled and sat up. "Hi, Travis. Decided to go swimming, huh?"

Travis always found it puzzling to talk to Kathy. With other guys she acted normal enough, but around him she'd get flustered and say something strange—like asking someone at a swimming pool if he'd decided to go swimming.

"Yeah, right," he said.

"My hair's such a mess," she said, trying to use her fingers as a comb to make it look better.

"It's okay." He paused. "You know what, Kathy, I like the color of your hair."

She smiled. "You do?"

"Sure."

"It's really snarly now."

"It just looks like you went swimming, but that's what you'd expect here. I can't stand girls who come here and never go swimming and just lie around putting suntan oil on all day. Why would they even come here, if they weren't going to get wet?"

"I agree," Kathy said, happy she'd gone in the water just a few minutes earlier.

Suddenly Travis stopped talking. He was staring at a group of young girls playing in the shallow end.

"Is something wrong?" she asked. She had never seen him look so troubled.

"Eleven years old . . ."

"Travis?"

"Sorry. I was thinking about something else. I think I'll go swim laps."

Kathy watched him swim. He was swimming the American crawl stroke, keeping his head in the water as much as possible, his head turning to the side for air. Sometimes just part of his mouth was out of the water as he breathed. She couldn't see how he could swim that way.

Half an hour passed. The threat of an approaching thunderstorm forced many swimmers to leave. Alan stopped Travis and told him he was going home. Travis nodded and continued swimming.

Kathy wanted the storm to hit because she knew the pool would have to close, and maybe she'd get a chance to talk to Travis and try to find out what was bothering him.

But the storm slipped past, and the pool stayed open, although by then most everyone had left.

But Travis kept swimming.

*Travis,* Kathy thought, *if there's something wrong, just tell me. I care about you more than you'll ever know. Please talk to me.*

But Travis kept swimming, his lean body gliding from one end of the pool to the other, alone, out of touch, in his own little troubled world.

*Please come out of the water,* Kathy thought.

Travis didn't want to stop. He wanted to go on and on until his body ached and he didn't have enough energy to think about what had happened to Sara, beginning when she was only eleven years old.

When her mother pulled into the parking lot and

honked, Kathy stood up and watched Travis one last time. *Something's very wrong*, she thought. Her mother honked again. Kathy sighed, picked up her towel, and went out to the car.

Travis kept swimming.

THAT AFTERNOON Joan and Sara waited in the outer office for Sara to see the psychologist assigned by the state.

"It's going to be okay," Joan said.

"What if he says I'm crazy?"

Joan smiled. "Just tell him I drove you to it."

The door opened, and a man came out to greet them. He was middle-aged, with a small mustache. He wore a gray suit that only approximately fitted him, but that fact didn't seem to bother him at all. He introduced himself as Vernon Collins.

Sara had never known anyone named Vernon before. She wondered what she was supposed to call him. She wasn't sure she could call him Vernon.

Joan excused herself, saying she was going to get some groceries. The psychologist suggested that she return in an hour. He invited Sara to come with him. She followed him inside, and he shut the door. There was no desk in the room, just two cushioned chairs facing each other.

"Please sit down," he said.

She sat down.

"I'm here to help you." He paused. "It might be a good idea for you to tell me a little more about yourself."

"Well, my name is Sara Corwin. I'll be a sophomore in high school when I start again. I have a dog named Muffin. He's a miniature poodle. I like to read. That's about it."

"Why are you here today?"

She gulped. "Didn't they tell you?"

"Yes, of course."

"Then why do I have to tell you?"

"You don't. I was just wondering if you could." He looked down at his pad of paper. "I'm told you're the victim of sexual abuse by your stepfather and that you're pregnant."

"Yes."

"Would you like to tell me about it?"

"I don't know if I could or not."

"I understand. Look, let me describe what we're going to do on your visits here. It's like having a room in your mind full of bad memories. If you want to clean it out, you first have to open the door, but sometimes when the things behind the door are horrible memories, opening that mental door is very hard. Maybe at first you'll want to open it just a tiny crack. Well, that's all right. We've got lots of time. But our goal is for you to open the door all the way and throw out all the garbage that's been hidden behind it. Then you can move on with your life. You'd like that, wouldn't you?"

"Yes."

"Whatever you feel comfortable in saying will be fine."

Sara swallowed, looked at Mr. Collins, and took a deep breath. "It first started when I was eleven . . ."


WHEN TRAVIS GOT HOME from swimming, his mother was talking on the phone. He made himself a bologna sandwich and sat down to read the latest issue of *National Geographic*. It wasn't a magazine he would have chosen for himself, but his dad made sure they always subscribed to it. Back issues, going back twenty or so years, were all stored in the basement, boxed according to the year. Travis usually glanced through each issue. Sometimes there'd be a picture of a place he would like to visit, or a map he could use to get extra credit from his teachers.

His mother got off the phone. "Travis," she said in a tone reserved for complaints, "the lunch meat is for lunch, not for snacks."

"I know, but I'm hungry."

"Have a peanut-butter sandwich, then."

Travis didn't argue. Sometimes lately he felt that there was another person living inside him, not as agreeable as the Travis of old. He was afraid to let his parents see the new version of himself; around them he acted the way they expected. But he wasn't sure how much longer he could keep the other Travis hidden.

"How was your day?" his mother asked.

"It was okay."

"Did you finish the work your father asked you to do?"

"Yes."

"I see your wet swimming suit and towel are still in the living room."

"I'll rinse them out and put 'em out to dry," he said in the monotone he used when forced to say what his mother wanted him to say.

"You went swimming?" she asked.

"Yeah."

"Who'd you go with?"

"Alan."

"Did you have a good time?"

"It was okay." He paused. "I swam four miles."

His mother wasn't paying attention. "That's nice. Oh, I took your father to the airport, so there'll be just the two of us for supper. Anything special you'd like?"

"Pizza."

"We had pizza three nights ago."

"So?"

"We can't have it all the time. How about a nice tuna salad?"

He sighed. He could never understand why mothers loved tuna. "I suppose."

"All right. Oh, I need to go out tonight. Your dad might call. If he does, tell him President Peterson wants him to phone as soon as possible." Travis's father served as President Peterson's first counselor in the stake presidency.

"Okay."

At eight o'clock his father called long distance. By then his mother had left. "Travis, how are you doing?"

"Fine. Mom's not here."

"That's okay. How are things back there? You holding down the fort okay?"

"Yeah, I guess so." His father always said that about the fort.

There was a long pause. "You say your mom's not home?"

"No, but she said you're supposed to call President Peterson."

"I wonder what he wants. Well, guess I'd better call him. Remember who you are, son."

"Yeah, sure, Dad. Bye." His father always told him to remember who he was. Travis knew that it really meant "don't mess up."

After hanging up, he made himself another bologna sandwich, hurrying to get it finished before his mother returned. Then he worked some more on his song for Sara. It still wasn't good enough.

# Chapter Five

THE NEXT MORNING while his mother was on campus, Travis went out to the backyard. He wanted to talk to Sara. To make sure she knew he was there, he mowed the lawn even though it didn't need it.

Sara heard the noise, saw him, and came out. He turned off the mower.

"Hi," he said.

"Hi."

"Want a bologna sandwich?" he asked.

"It's too early. I just ate breakfast."

They sat down in the lawn chairs.

"Did you see the state car here yesterday?" she asked.

"Yeah."

"They took my statement. They're going to arrest Dillon real soon. They said he'll probably post bail. I'm glad he can't find where I'm staying. But I'm worried about Muffin. What if Dillon takes it out on him?"

"He won't."

"You don't know Dillon like I do. He might hurt Muffin just out of spite. I think we should try to get Muffin out of there."

"How?"

"We could call Diane in Ogden. She's a friend of mine. We could ask her to keep Muffin for me."

"Okay."

"After all Joan and Gary are doing for me, I don't

feel right asking to charge calls on their phone, but I've got to call Diane and ask her to help." She paused. "Will you loan me some money for the call until I can pay you back?"

"How much?"

"Maybe a couple of dollars."

"I guess so."

"Thanks. And could you go with me to make the call in case it costs more than that?"

"All right. When?"

She thought about it. "I hate to be a bother, but could we do it after I finish the jobs Joan's lined up for me?"

"Sure, no problem."

After Sara finished her work, they rode the ten-speeds to a convenience store near the outskirts of town. Travis got two dollars' worth of change from the woman behind the counter.

The pay phone was outside. Travis wasn't interested in hearing Sara talk to Diane about Muffin, so he went inside and bought two candy bars, then walked over to the magazine rack and began reading a sports magazine.

"You going to buy that?" the woman asked.

"Probably not."

"This isn't a library, you know."

He put the magazine down.

A few minutes later Sara came inside. "I need some more money or the operator is going to cut me off."

He hesitated.

"Please, Travis, I'm almost finished."

He wondered if she knew he'd always give in to her. He handed her two one-dollar bills.

"Thanks. This really means a lot to me." She got change from the woman, then hurried back to the pay phone.

*Four dollars for a dog,* he thought. *I must be going crazy.*

He ate one of the candy bars, then without thinking ate the other one which he'd gotten for Sara. That made him feel selfish, so he bought two more.

He went outside to wait for her. When she hung up, she was very happy. "We got it all worked out. Diane'll get Muffin tomorrow night when my folks are out bowling. She'll keep him at her place until we can make arrangements to ship him up here." She paused. "There's just one more thing."

"What's that?"

"Diane says she'll need money for dog food. I said I'd mail her some."

"Sara, why all this fuss for a dog?"

"He's more to me than just a dog. You don't know what it was like for me. Muffin was the only one I could turn to. There was nobody else."

He sighed. "How much do you need?"

"Five dollars."

"I'll loan it to you."

She touched him on the arm. "Thanks a million, Travis."

He gave her a candy bar. There was a picnic table next to the store, so they sat down and ate and enjoyed the warm sunny day.

"Joan says I'm part of the family now, so I have to pull my share. She made up a list of chores for me to do. I don't mind. She's such a character. She sings like an opera singer whenever she vacuums. It's great to be with her. I used to pray to God I could be in a normal family, and now I am." She stopped. "What are you looking at?"

She'd caught him. "You."

"Why?"

"I like to look at your face."

"You might not want to when I get big."

"It won't make any difference."

"We'll see."

"I mean it, Sara."

"I'm lucky to have you for a friend."

When they returned home, Joan invited Travis to stay for lunch. While Sara went to change clothes and wash up, Travis sat in the kitchen and made funny faces for the kids. He liked to make them giggle because he thought children's giggles were the best sound in the whole world.

Joan's house wasn't as neat as the one Travis came from, but it was more fun. Joan was writing a roadshow for the ward, and she'd been making up songs all day for it. To Travis, she seemed orange in a world of gray.

Joan made sloppy joes while she talked on the phone to her co-writer for the roadshow. Eventually she hung up and turned her attention to Travis. "Travis, thanks for taking Sara under your wing."

"Sure."

"You understand why she's staying with us, don't you?"

"Yeah, she told me."

"I just wanted to be sure. She went through a lot of bad times before she came here. Having a baby and going through a trial is going to be hard for her too. So it's nice she has a friend like you."

Sara came into the kitchen.

"Sara, hon, can you set the table for us?" Joan asked.

"Okay."

When lunch was ready, they had a blessing on the food and sat down to eat. Afterwards Joan had to work some more on the roadshow. As soon as she left the kitchen, Sara handed Travis an envelope with Diane's address on it. "Can you put the money in here and mail it today?"

"Okay."

"Thanks, Travis."

While Sara cleared the table, Travis went to the family room with the kids to watch TV. After a while that got boring, so he went back to the kitchen. Sara was doing dishes and listening to songs on the radio. He tiptoed up and, as a joke, put his hands over her eyes. Instinctively she brought her elbow back and hit him in the stomach.

The blow bent him over double and left him gasping for breath.

"Oh, Travis!" Sara cried out. "I'm sorry. I hurt you, didn't I? I'm so sorry. I can't stand to have someone sneak up on me. It reminds me of Dillon. Oh, he made such a mess out of me!" She ran to her room and shut the door.

Travis waited for her but after a while, when she didn't come out, he went home and sat down at the piano and worked on his song for her. Once again it all came out wrong. He kept thinking of the harm Dillon had done, and it made him furious. He played "Toccata and Fugue in D Minor" by Bach. He made it sound like a thunderstorm of music. That was the way he felt, and he played it again and again.

His mother came home. "I'm about to go get your father at the airport. Want to come along?"

"I guess so."

Travis thought it strange that around him his mother referred to her husband as "your father." He wondered if he'd ever call his wife "your mother" to his kids.

He went to his room and got a five-dollar bill, stuck it in Sara's envelope, sealed it, and slipped it into his front jeans pocket.

"Can I drive the car out of the driveway?" he asked. She said yes. He liked driving. In the fall he was scheduled to take driver's training, and then he could get a license.

As they drove to the airport, his mother commented, "I wonder what your father brought us."

Travis recalled a time when he had eagerly awaited his father's return, when each trip meant a new toy and whatever bags of airplane peanuts his father had saved up during the trip. But he'd outgrown all that. He'd never told his father that, because he was afraid that if he did, the presents might stop.

"Travis, your father really wishes he could spend more time with you. He's so busy these days with marketing CATTLE-1."

"Mom, what does CATTLE-1 do? Somebody asked me once and I don't know."

"Your father says it's a way to use a computer so that a rancher can increase his income."

"How does it do that?"

She paused. "Maybe we should have him explain it to us."

"Okay. Can I turn on the radio?"

She sighed. "If you must."

Travis found a song he liked and looked out the window.

In Travis's eyes, the Logan airport wasn't much of an airport, especially compared to the one in Salt Lake City where they sometimes took his father. A shuttle plane came to Logan from Salt Lake a couple of times a day. The small plane looked like a cigar with wings. When the passengers emerged, they would come out hunched over because of the low door and cramped interior. To Travis, it always looked like the plane had arrived from the land of the Munchkins.

While they waited for the plane to land, Travis spotted a mailbox. Making sure his mother wouldn't notice, he pulled out the crumpled envelope from his pocket and slipped it into the mailbox.

The plane was on time. Travis's father walked

quickly inside the terminal, hugged his wife, and said hello to Travis. Travis was by then at the point where any show of affection from his parents was embarrassing.

"Here's some peanuts," his father said, emptying his suit pockets. "And I got something else for you too."

Travis opened the small package.

"Know what it is?" his father asked.

"No."

"It's a gyroscope. They're used as navigational aids for ships and planes and missiles. It's very scientific. I'll show you how it works when we get home."

"Thanks," Travis said, trying to be enthusiastic.

"You're welcome."

They had to wait for his father's suitcase. "Well, what's been going on while I've been gone?"

"Did you call President Peterson?" his mother asked.

"Yes, we're having a special high council meeting tonight."

The baggage showed up and they walked out to the car. It was always assumed that his father would drive, even when his mother had driven there. Travis got in the back seat.

"Well, I've got some really exciting news," his father said, as they pulled out of the airport parking lot. "After I presented my paper at the meeting, I met with some Japanese cattlemen. They're very interested in what I'm doing. There's a possibility I'll be invited to Japan next month to work with them. They said they'd provide me with an extra ticket for a family member to accompany me."

"Oh, Howard, that's wonderful! Take Travis."

"Not me," Travis said quickly. "I don't want to go to Japan."

"Why not?" his father asked.

"They eat raw fish and talk funny."

His father smiled. "I'm sure they have a McDonald's there somewhere, so you wouldn't starve."

"Travis, go," his mother said. "It'll be a wonderful learning experience."

"Mom, you never go anywhere with Dad. You go with him and I'll take care of things here."

"Oh no," she said. "I've got all these summer school classes to finish up."

"I'm sure your instructors would be willing to work out some kind of arrangement so you could go," his father said.

"Well, even so, Travis should go. You and he need more time together. Besides, it'd be such a valuable educational experience for him."

Travis didn't think he could stand an educational trip with his father. He pictured them going around visiting Japanese gyroscope factories. "Mom, I really don't want to go."

"Well," his father said, "there's really not much use planning anything until we see if they're serious about bringing me over."

"Oh, Howard, I'm happy for you. This means you're internationally recognized, doesn't it?"

His father was pleased at the compliment. "Well, nothing may come of it. We'll just have to see how it turns out."

They pulled into the driveway. His father got out, looked around the yard, and turned to Travis. "The front strip needs water."

After supper his father invited him into his office at home. "Your mother says you'd like to know more about CATTLE-1."

"Yeah, sort of."

"Sit down and I'll show you how it works. What I've

developed here is menu-driven range management software that a rancher can use to optimize his cattle operation."

He inserted the program disk into the disk reader. A few seconds later, the monitor flashed TASK SELECTION MENU. "Okay, now what do you want to do?"

Travis read the possibilities. "I don't know."

"Well, let's suppose you want to know when's the best time to sell your cattle. That's menu *b*. So push *b* and then push *Enter*."

His father kept asking questions and Travis kept getting the answers wrong. Finally, feeling very frustrated, he said, "Dad, I think I get the main idea. Can I go out and change the sprinkler now? I'm doing the front strip like you said."

"Sure, go ahead."

Travis went outside. Next door Sara and Joan were in the kitchen doing dishes, enthusiastically belting out one of the songs Joan had written for the roadshow. When they were done, Gary and the kids gave them a standing ovation.

# Chapter Six

LATE THAT NIGHT Sara sat in her room with the lights out. This time she wasn't afraid of Dillon. This time she was afraid of herself.

She'd hit Travis.

Dillon had hit her, and now she'd hit Travis.

Dillon had beat her up so many times. It was no good when she wouldn't cooperate because first he'd beat her up, then go out and get drunk, then come home and beat her mother, and then start on her again. After all that, he always got his way anyway. And so to save her mother from being beat up, she had learned to give up without a fight. Dillon didn't need a gun to get what he wanted. Being in the role of her father was gun enough.

Dillon had hit her, and now she'd hit Travis.

She touched a scar on her back. It was one of the wounds Dillon had given her the night he'd beat her with a golf club. After gym class last year, while other girls got dressed facing the lockers, she dressed with her back to the lockers, so nobody would be able to see her scars.

She could live with the scars on her back, but it was the scars in her mind that worried her the most. She had read once that children who have been physically abused as children often grow up to abuse their own children. She was terrified of that. Even now she dreaded the times when Joan left her alone to babysit, because she was afraid the children might do something to make her

54

angry, and, without thinking, she might lose control and hit one of them. She never had, but she felt that she had to be careful all the time.

Dillon had hit her, and if she wasn't careful, she might end up someday, out of control, beating her children. And yet she loved kids. More than anything, she wanted to be a wife and a mother. She worried that maybe she had been so hurt by Dillon that the things she wanted most in life—a husband, a marriage, and children—were the things she couldn't have.

Sara didn't go out in the kitchen that night, for fear that Joan would wake up and ask what was bothering her. She couldn't tell anyone about this now, not even Vernon Collins.

"THERE'S A BOY NEXT DOOR," Sara said to Vernon Collins at their next session. "His name is Travis. We went hiking once. He loaned me some money so I can get Muffin away from my stepfather." She paused. "He knows about me and everything, but he still says he wants to be friends. One time when I was crying, he put his arm around me, and I wasn't afraid or worried. I'm usually so jumpy around guys, but he's different. I feel safe with him. Better than safe even. I feel comfortable and, you know, like everything's going to be all right. Except yesterday when he sneaked up behind me and scared me and I hit him in the stomach with my elbow. I felt really ashamed about that."

"Ashamed?" Vernon asked.

"It's because of what Dillon did to me that I'm so jumpy." She paused. "I can't understand why Travis keeps coming around."

"Why's that?"

"He's too good for me."

"I take it you think you're not good?"

"That's right. I'm not good."

"Why do you say that?"

"Because of what happened to me."

"I thought we agreed that what happened to you wasn't your fault."

She paused. "Yes, I guess we did."

"Then why do you say you're not a good person?"

She paused. "I'm not ready to open that door yet."

"All right, we'll wait. How do you feel about the things we've talked about so far?"

"It's been good. It's like taking a heavy load off me."

"Of course it's not all going to clear up overnight. We just have to keep working at it, but I'm pleased with the progress you're making."


JUST AFTER NOON, as soon as she got home from seeing Vernon Collins, Sara went out to find Travis. He was weeding the garden. Sara felt good. She was in the mood for fun. She turned on the hose in the Townsends' backyard, sneaked over to the hedge, and sprayed Travis with water.

He howled in protest, but a big smile spread over his face. Vowing revenge, he went to his hose. Soon they had a full-scale water fight, with Joan and her three kids involved in it too. Within a short time everyone was drenched. After they changed their clothes, Sara fixed ice cream cones.

Later that day Joan had to go to the mall. She invited Sara and Travis to go along. At the mall she took her children into a store, leaving Sara and Travis free to walk around. Just as they passed a clothing store, Kathy came out. They nearly bumped into each other. "Hi, Kathy," Travis said.

Kathy stared at Sara. "Hello," she said coolly.

Both girls waited for Travis to make the introductions. Finally he took the hint. "Sara, this is Kathy."

"Hi," the two girls said.

"Sara is staying with the Townsends next door."

"Oh," Kathy said.

"We're here with Joan and her kids," Travis said.

"Oh."

"See you around, Kathy."

"Nice meeting you," Sara said.

"Yes."

They left Kathy. Sara didn't say anything for a while.

"Is something wrong?" he asked.

"Kathy likes you a lot, doesn't she."

"Not really. She and I are just friends."

"Maybe so, but I got the feeling she didn't like me being with you."

When they got home, Travis excused himself. "I'd better go put my wet clothes in the dryer before my mother gets home and finds out about the water fight."

"What difference does it make if she does find out?"

He shrugged. "None, I guess."

"Then why are you trying to cover it up?"

"I don't want my parents knowing everything that happens to me."

"Why not?"

"Because they're always asking me why I do things. Sometimes I don't know why. Why do they think I have to have a reason?"

"What's the worst thing you ever did that your parents found out about?" she asked.

"One time I told my parents I was going to bed, but then instead I sneaked out and went with some friends for a pizza. My dad checked on me a few minutes later and knew I'd left. When I came home, he was there waiting."

"Did he hit you?"

"No."

"Did he ground you for a month?"

"No."

"What did he do?"

"He told me he was disappointed in me."

"That's it?"

"He said I didn't need to go sneaking around in the middle of the night. He said, 'If you wanted to go out for a pizza, then you should've asked us.'"

"So what's so bad about that?"

"It's just that he always makes me feel like I should've known better. It's like he won't let me be a kid; he wants me to be the way he is. But I'm not sure I want to be like him. All he ever does is work."

"I don't see what your problem is, Travis. It sounds to me like you've got great folks."

"But they don't know anything about me anymore. Instead of telling 'em how I really feel, I just tell 'em what they want to hear. Most of the time they don't have the slightest idea what I'm thinking."

"Then why don't you tell 'em?"

He paused. "Because they couldn't just let it be. They'd keep nagging and preaching until I couldn't stand it anymore."

"What are these deep dark secrets you don't want your parents to know about?"

He cleared his throat. "What do you mean?"

"What are the things you hide from your parents?"

"That's not a fair question."

"Why isn't it? You know all about me."

He hesitated. "One of them is that I'm not sure I want to go on a mission for the Church."

"What else?"

"I'm tired of taking piano lessons. I want to quit."

"Why don't you quit, then?"

"Because my mother wants me to keep taking lessons."

"I think you should tell her how you feel."

"She wouldn't like it."

"Maybe not, but at least she'd know."

"I suppose."

Sara smiled. "Hey, maybe I could take you along with me to see my psychologist. Vernon Collins is his name. He'd get a big kick out of talking to you."

"I don't want to see a psychologist. I'm not crazy."

"You don't have to be crazy to see a psychologist. Take me, for instance."

"Yeah, right," Travis snickered. Sara faked being angry and lightly popped him with a cushion from a lawn chair.

SOON AFTER TRAVIS WENT HOME, his mother returned from her classes. The dryer buzzed. "Are you doing laundry?" she asked.

"Yeah. A shirt and a pair of jeans and some underwear and socks."

"What for?"

"I needed something to wear tonight."

"You've got plenty of clothes in your closet."

Travis played dumb. "I do?"

"Of course. I did laundry yesterday."

"Oh."

Travis got his dry clothes out of the dryer and folded them the way his mother liked him to do. Afterwards he practiced the piano.

Later that night, after his parents were gone, Travis

worked on Sara's song. It had to be just right because it was her song. Someday he'd play it for her, and then she'd know how much he cared about her.

KATHY SPENT THE EVENING in her room on the phone, trying to get information about the girl staying with the Townsends, but nobody seemed to know anything.

*Who is she?* Kathy agonized. *And why is she staying with the Townsends? Is she Sister Townsend's niece? But if she is, why doesn't she go to church? I can't let her just walk in and take Travis away from me.*

That night the memories of Travis wouldn't come. Instead she tortured herself with the image of this interloper, this girl with blond hair and unforgettable blue eyes, this girl who walked so comfortably alongside Travis.

*It's not fair,* she thought.

# Chapter Seven

A FEW DAYS LATER Travis's father phoned from the office to excitedly announce he had been officially invited to Japan for two weeks in July. There would also be an extra ticket provided for a family member.

That night Travis tried his best to talk his mother into going. "But where would you stay while we're gone?" she asked him.

His father had an answer. "We could have Travis stay on the farm with Uncle Bert."

That was the last thing on the earth Travis wanted. If he stayed with Uncle Bert on his farm in Idaho, he'd end up working his head off without getting paid a dime. "If I stayed with Uncle Bert, who'd take care of our lawn and garden?" Travis countered.

"We'd hire somebody. One of your friends."

"Let me do it, Dad. I need the money. I could stay with Alan's family. They'd take me in, I know they would."

His father paused. "Well, I don't know. Two weeks is a long time."

"I'd be okay, honest."

"We'll see."

The next several days in the Fitzgerald family was a time of list making. Travis realized he was on both his parents' lists—what to do with Travis. He tried to be a model son so he wouldn't be forced to stay with Uncle Bert.

"Are you sure you'd be all right staying with Alan?" his mother asked.

"I'd be fine."

Finally his parents agreed to let him stay in Logan.

On July 5, the day of departure, President Peterson offered to take his parents to the airport in Salt Lake City, since he had to go there for business anyway. So Travis would bid his parents farewell when they dropped him off at Alan's.

That morning on the way to Alan's house, his mother was still going over her list with him. "Travis, you will change your underwear every day, won't you?"

"Mother," he grumbled, wishing she'd stop prying into his private life.

"Hygiene is very important. And promise me you'll wear socks."

"I will."

"Do you have a key to the house?" his father asked.

"It's in my pocket."

"Do you know what to do with the mail?"

Travis couldn't believe his father would ask him that. "Take it in every day."

"Right. The thing is to make the house look like there's people living there," his father said. "If you let three or four days' worth of newspapers pile up on the porch, thieves'll know there's nobody there. Keep that in mind."

"I will."

His mother continued. "Whatever Alan's mother asks you to do, you do it. And once in a while offer to do the dishes after supper. Keep asking her what you can do to help."

When they arrived at Alan's house, the two women conversed while Travis and Alan carted his stuff into the house. His father stayed in the car and stared at his watch. "Ruth, we've got five minutes before President Peterson is scheduled to pick us up at home."

When Travis came out after taking his things in, his mother smothered him with a hug. His father got out and shook his hand. "Remember who you are, son."

"I will, Dad."

A minute later they were both gone.

Travis was relieved.

THE DAY AFTER HIS PARENTS LEFT, while he was home mowing the lawn, Sara came over to see him.

He turned off the mower.

"I just got a letter from Diane. She sent back your money. Here it is. She said her dad wouldn't let her take Muffin. He said it would be like stealing, and he wouldn't let her do it. But she did walk by the front yard and saw Muffin there. She said he looked okay."

"So it's not as bad as you thought."

"Maybe not. Except I miss him so much."

"Sure."

"Travis, you'd really love Muffin. He's the smartest and best dog in the whole world."

IT WAS PAST MIDNIGHT. Alan, sprawled on the grass in his sleeping bag, was sound asleep. Next to him, Travis lay awake, thinking how much Sara loved Muffin. Her birthday was in four days. Bringing her Muffin would be the best gift he could possibly give her. He wished he had a driver's license and his own car, because then he'd drive to Ogden and bring Muffin back with him. But he didn't have a car, and he didn't have a driver's license.

But he did have a ten-speed.

THE NEXT DAY Travis went to see Sara. He rang the doorbell. "Come in," Joan called out. He walked in. Sara and Joan were hunched over a sewing machine. "Look at this girl," Joan bragged, "making her own clothes."

Sara showed what she'd done so far. "It looks more like a tent. It's a dress for my last few months of being pregnant."

As Travis watched Sara, he could tell she was glad she knew how to run a sewing machine. In a minute she came to the end of one part of the job.

"Want to help me change the hose?" Travis asked.

"Joan, is it okay if I stop for a second?"

"Sure, go ahead. I'll try and decide what we're having for supper." She grinned. "Gary always likes to know details like that when he comes home. He's such a slave driver."

"If you ask me," Travis teased, "I think he puts up with a lot."

"You scoundrel," Joan said, faking outrage. "Out of my house this instant."

Travis and Sara walked over to his backyard. "You said you used to live in Ogden. What was your address?"

She told him. "Why do you want to know?"

"Just curious."

ON JULY 8, the day before Sara's birthday, Travis got up very early in the morning, left a note for Alan's parents saying he was going for a bike ride, and then walked to his home. There he made sandwiches and filled a canteen, put it in a daypack, knelt down and said a prayer, then set out on his ten-speed for Ogden, fifty miles away.

The day before, he'd worried about how he could carry Muffin on a ten-speed. After rummaging around, he finally came up with an idea he thought would work.

He'd put Muffin inside a daypack. He asked Sara how big Muffin was. From her description it seemed that he'd fit.

Just after daybreak he rode through the nearly deserted streets of Logan. Finally he reached the highway. There was a long uphill climb out of the valley and into Wellsville Canyon.

His journey had begun. This was for Sara. On the steep hills, when it took everything he had just to keep going, he thought of Sara. Each time the whoosh from a semitruck brushed him aside as if he were only a leaf in the wind, each time a motorist honked for him to move over, each time he wiped the beads of sweat from his forehead—he thought of Sara. For him this was a pure and noble adventure. He felt like a knight riding out in honor of his queen, on a heroic quest.

When he reached the summit he stopped and ate two bologna sandwiches and had some water. Then he started down the canyon into Brigham City.

At one-thirty that afternoon he reached Ogden. He stopped at a gas station to ask directions and found out he still had to pedal halfway across town. On the way there, he got lost and had to ask directions again. It wasn't until late in the afternoon that he stopped in front of the house where Sara used to live. It was a modest home in a neighborhood that had seen better times.

*So this is where a man lives who sexually abuses a girl,* he thought. It seemed wrong that it looked like the other houses on the block. It depressed him that it looked the same because it meant there might be other houses, even places he'd passed that very day, where girls were being abused. Maybe they hadn't told anyone about it yet, and so they were still having to suffer through the same awful things Sara had gone through. He wished he knew which houses they were so he could stop and tell each girl to see a teacher in school or a church leader or a police officer and tell them what was happening, so those awful things would stop once and for all.

Muffin was in the front yard, attached to a long rope so he had plenty of room to run around. *They treat their dog better than they treated Sara,* he thought.

Travis wasn't exactly sure what to do next. He rode to the end of the block and stopped and looked around. He was alone, so he closed his eyes and said a quiet prayer.

As he slowly walked his bicycle back to the house, he tried to decide what to do. He thought that this was somewhat like what they'd studied in seminary class, when Nephi tried to get the brass plates from Laban. At first Nephi tried the direct approach. Travis decided maybe that might be best for him too. He walked up to the door and rang the bell.

A tired-looking woman answered the door. Travis wanted to hate her, but instead he found himself feeling sorry for her because she'd lost Sara's love and respect. "Are you Sara's mother?" he asked.

"Sara doesn't live here anymore."

"I know. I'm a friend of hers where she's staying now. She wants her dog Muffin. I've come to take him to her."

"Where is she staying?"

"I can't tell you that."

"I need to talk some sense in her head before she ends up destroying her own family."

"Is it okay if I take Muffin to her?"

"No. Get out of here before I call the cops."

"Sara loves that dog."

"So?"

"Why don't you care about Sara?"

The woman paused. "Is that what you think?"

"You didn't stop what was going on. To me that means you didn't care about her."

"There was nothing going on."

"Yes there was, and you know it."

She wouldn't look at him. "Even if there was, it's no reason to try to send Dillon to jail. Then what'll happen to me? Tell her to come back and we'll pay for her to get an abortion if she'll drop the charges against Dillon."

At first Travis was going to argue but then decided against it. "I'll make a deal with you. I'll tell her that if you'll let me take Muffin." The woman hesitated. "Maybe Sara'll change her mind if I talk to her," Travis said, although he didn't believe it.

She shrugged. "All right, take the dog. He doesn't mean much to us. But you be sure and tell her what I said."

"I will. I promise."

Travis took Muffin, still tied to the rope, and left quickly before Sara's mother changed her mind. He stopped at a store and bought a small box of dog biscuits. He petted Muffin and gave him dog biscuits and tried to make friends with him. It took him a long time to finally get the dog coaxed into getting into the daypack. After he was in there, Travis repeatedly lifted it up and down, a little higher each time. He wanted Muffin to feel comfortable about being on his back.

When he was finally able to put Muffin on his back and start on his trip home, he kept looking back, to make sure Dillon wasn't following him. It wasn't until five o'clock that he finally got out of Ogden. On the highway it was slow traveling with Muffin on his back, but at least he had both hands freed up.

A little before ten o'clock that night Travis was still five miles from Logan. But he was grateful the last part of the trip was downhill. "Hey, Muffin, we're going to see Sara tonight!" It seemed to him that Muffin understood, because he barked.

Finally Travis arrived home. He got off his bicycle, sat down, and carefully removed the pack from his aching shoulders, then put the rope on Muffin and led him to the Townsends' front door. He rang the doorbell and called out, "Sara! Come here! I've got your birthday present."

When Sara came to the door, Muffin started barking. "Muffin!" she shrieked, rushing out the door, kneeling down, and throwing her arms around her pet. "Travis, this is the best birthday present I've ever had in my life." She came over and gave him a hug. Travis felt very good.

Joan and Gary came out. Instead of sharing Sara's happiness, they looked concerned. "Travis, did you tell Alan's parents where you were going today?" Gary asked.

"Well, sort of. Why?"

"Alan came by after supper looking for you. He said they didn't know where you were. They were worried you'd taken your bicycle up the canyon to go hiking and got hurt. I think you'd better get over there right away and let them know you're okay."

Travis hurried to Alan's place. As he rounded the corner, he saw a police car at the house. He leaned the ten-speed against the side of the garage and went to the front door. A policeman was sitting in the living room with Alan and his parents.

"Do you have any idea where he might have gone?" one of them asked.

Travis opened the screen door and walked in.

"Travis Fitzgerald!" Alan's mother yelled. "Where have you been?"

"I went to Ogden on my ten-speed."

"Do you have any idea how worried we've been about you?"

The policeman stood up. "I guess there's no need for me to be here now."

There was a big emotional scene after the police left. Alan's mother got hysterical. She told him all the ways someone on a ten-speed could die on a busy highway, and all the other terrible fates she had imagined.

"I was all right."

"Travis," Alan's father said, "we can't continue to keep you here if you cause us any more problems like today."

"I won't. Honest."

By the next day, due to Alan's big mouth, everyone knew about Travis's trip. Rumors were that it involved a girl named Sara, although nobody knew much about her except that she was staying with the Townsends.

For the rest of his stay, things remained tense between Travis and Alan's parents. He spent as much time as possible at home working on the lawn and garden and helping Sara build a doghouse for Muffin. It was while they were working on the doghouse that he finally gave Sara the message from her mother.

"I could never get an abortion," she said. "What happened to me isn't the baby's fault. I can't just do away with my baby because it's not convenient to have it. To me that would be wrong."

"I knew you'd say that," Travis said proudly.

For the next few days, whenever Travis had spare time at home, he went to the piano and worked on his song for Sara. By then he had a snatch of a melody. It was a love song, but for some reason, even then, it made him sad to hear it.

# Chapter Eight

"REMEMBER ME TELLING YOU about Travis, the boy who lives next door?" Sara asked Vernon Collins at their next session. "Well, two days ago he rode his bicycle all the way to Ogden, to where my mom and Dillon live, and he talked my mom into letting me have my dog Muffin. Then he rode all the way back with Muffin inside a backpack. I just can't believe that anyone would do that for me."

"Why do you think he did it?" Vernon Collins asked.

"Because he knows how much I love Muffin. He said it was my birthday present."

"He must care about you a great deal to have done that."

She paused. "I don't know, maybe so."

"How do you feel about him?"

"He's a nice guy. I mean, you can just look at him and tell. He has this really innocent boyish face. He doesn't even think bad thoughts, and he doesn't swear, not at all. I think his biggest secret from his parents is that he doesn't want to take piano lessons anymore."

"Why do you think he likes you?"

She shook her head. "I don't know. It doesn't make sense."

"Why do you say that?"

"Because he's good, and I'm not."

"Can you tell me why you feel that way when we've already agreed that what happened wasn't your fault?"

She didn't answer. Mr. Collins waited.

"Deep inside I still feel it was my fault," she finally said.

"In what way?"

"Dillon told me he couldn't help himself when he saw me looking flirty."

"I'm curious—what did you do to look flirty?"

She shrugged. "I don't know. I never knew what he was talking about."

"Did you wear skimpy clothes around him?"

"No."

"What do you suppose you did, then?"

"Dillon said it was just the way I was."

"What did he mean by that?"

She paused. "One time I saw this movie about this girl who had evil powers, and people couldn't help but do what she wanted them to do. Even bad things. That's the way Dillon talked about me—like I sent out these signals and he couldn't help himself."

"Has Travis ever told you he has sexual feelings for you that he can't control?"

She shook her head. "Travis isn't like that."

"Have you ever considered that maybe it wasn't you looking flirty? Maybe it was Dillon. Maybe he had a dirty mind. Maybe whenever he looked at girls, he thought dirty thoughts regardless of what they wore or did."

"I see what you're trying to get at, but I still feel guilty."

"Are there any other reasons why you might feel guilty?"

She paused. "I guess I'm not ready to talk about that yet."

TRAVIS'S PARENTS ARRIVED HOME from their Japan trip on July 17. They were not yet aware of Travis's trip to Ogden, although almost everyone else in the neighborhood was. Alan had seen to that, and in doing so, he had stirred up great curiosity about this Sara who had mysteriously turned up at the Townsends'. He had pestered Travis for details, but Travis wouldn't tell him a thing.

When Travis's parents showed up to pick him up, Alan's mother ran out to the car and began pouring out her complaints about what she'd gone through with their son. Travis gathered his things in Alan's room. He dreaded having to face his parents.

"Why won't you tell me about Sara?" Alan asked

"Because if I do, you'll tell everybody."

"She must really be something for you to ride all the way to Ogden and back just to get her stupid dog. Have you ever kissed her?"

Travis scowled. "Grow up, Alan, okay?"

"I bet you have but you don't want to talk about it. How many times? Or have there been so many you've lost track?"

There was no response from Travis.

"All right, let's try this—smile if you've kissed her."

Travis shook his head. "Alan, you're an idiot."

After Alan's mother had unloaded all her frustrations on Travis's parents, she came inside. "Travis," she said, her voice strangely formal, "your parents are here to take you home."

Travis picked up his things. "Thanks for letting me stay here."

"Don't try to butter me up. I've already told your parents what happened. They'll be talking to you about it when you get home."

Travis went outside and got in the car. "How was Japan?" he asked.

"From what Alan's mother says, it looks like we never should have gone," his mother said.

It was a tense ride home. Just before they pulled into the driveway, his father said, "Help us get unpacked, Travis, and then we'll have a family council."

They all carried in luggage. A few minutes later they sat down in the dining room for a family council.

"Travis," his father said, "Alan's mother said you ran away without leaving word, and that you were gone all day and most of the night. Finally she got so worried she called the police. They were about to organize a search-and-rescue team to go looking for you in the mountains when you showed up. What do you have to say for yourself?"

"I don't see what the problem was. I left her a note saying I was going on a bicycle ride."

"Yes, but she thought you'd just be a couple of hours. When you didn't come back all day, she thought you'd been killed or injured."

"She shouldn't have worried. I was okay."

"Where did you go?"

"To Ogden."

"Ogden? What for?"

"To get Sara's dog."

"Who's Sara?" his father asked.

"The girl living with the Townsends."

"Travis," his mother complained, "I wrote you a detailed list of what we expected while we were gone. Did you even read it?"

"Sure, I read it."

"But that didn't stop you from running all over the country, did it?"

"I went to Ogden, Mom. That's not all over the country."

"Well," his father said, "I can see we'll have to wait before we give you the gift we bought you. We'll just have to see if we can get a little more obedience from you."

Travis was angry that his father thought he could bribe him with some trinket from Japan, which later, to Travis's disappointment, turned out to be an educational book about the Japanese art of paper folding.

"Why would you go all that way for a dog?" his father asked.

"Sara missed it a lot, and besides, she was afraid of what her stepfather would do to the dog."

"Why would her stepfather hurt her dog?"

"Because she's pressing charges against him for sexual abuse."

"Good grief," his father said. "What's this neighborhood coming to that my son should be learning things like this?"

"Travis, how do you feel about this girl?" his mother asked.

"Sara's the best friend I've ever had."

His parents looked at each other in alarm.


THE NEXT DAY Travis's mother went next door to visit. Afterwards she stopped off at at her husband's office on campus. "Well, I met her," she said.

"What's she like?"

"She's a good-looking girl with blond hair and blue-green eyes. Her eyes are her best feature. There's kind of a haunting sadness to them. I imagine it's very appealing to a boy like Travis. I talked to Joan. She said Sara's a foster child, placed by the state. Her stepfather sexually abused her. She was taken from her home when it was discovered she was pregnant."

"The girl's pregnant?"

"Yes."

"Does she look it?"

"Not yet."

"What do you make of Travis's involvement with her?"

"I'm not sure. He seems very committed to her. Why else would he ride to Ogden on a bike just to get her dog?"

"Is she a member of the Church?"

"No."

"Do you think we should tell him to stop seeing her?"

"I don't think so. It might drive them closer together. Let's face it, the girl doesn't have anything to lose. After all she's been through, she might be looking for someone like Travis to marry."

"What do you suggest we do, then?"

"I think we should invite Sara over for supper."


"OH, NO! THIS IS AWFUL!" Sara cried out. "Joan, come here! I can't wear this! It's horrible!"

"Let me look at it," Joan said, coming in to see what Sara had just finished sewing. The hemline was crooked and had puckered up into uneven folds.

"I should never have said I'd go," Sara said.

"Don't worry. We can fix it."

"Maybe you can, but I can't."

"Go in the kitchen and get us both some diet soda and ice while I see what I can do."

Sara went to the kitchen and got their drinks, and then returned to watch Joan. She found herself fascinated with Joan's hands. They could work wonders. Twice while she worked, her children interrupted her. Joan stopped, soothed, touched, caressed, kissed hurts to make them better, encouraged, hugged, and sent

them on their way, and all the time she assured Sara that
her dress, the one she'd wear when she ate supper with
Travis and his family, would be fine.

"Okay, try it on," Joan said half an hour later.

Sara tried on the dress and looked in the mirror. It
looked much better. "Oh, Joan, thanks. You're so wonderful. How will I ever be able to repay you for all you're
doing for me?"

"Someday when you're older and more secure, look
around. Maybe there'll be someone you can help. Is it a
deal?"

"I'll never be as good at helping people as you are."

Joan laughed. "Hey, I'm just making this up as I go
along." She put her hands on Sara's shoulders. "Now
look, hon, you're going to turn out just fine. Don't let
anyone ever tell you you're not, okay?" She gave Sara a
hug and went back to her work.

Sara tried to sew, but her tears kept getting in the
way.


THE NEXT DAY Sara ate supper with Travis and his parents.

"Sara," Travis's father said, "before we have our evening meal, we usually kneel for family prayer."

"Joan and Gary do that too."

They all knelt down.

"Travis, will you offer our prayer?" his father asked.

As they started dinner, everything proceeded
smoothly at first. Sara appreciated the way Travis's parents treated her. Much of the conversation clung to safe
topics—the weather, hiking, CATTLE-1, observations
about Japan from their recent trip.

"What year will you be in school?" Travis's father
asked.

Sara hesitated. "Travis and I will both be sophomores, but I won't be attending high school until after I have the baby. That'll be in January."

"I see."

"Although they'll give me some material to work on at home."

"That's good," Travis's mother said. "I say it's always better to keep your mind busy. You know, I've just started college again after not doing anything for years, and believe me, it's been tough to get my mind working again."

"What are your favorite subjects in school?" Travis's father asked.

"I like to read. And I like math."

"I loved math as a boy too, and of course, Travis is very good at math too, aren't you."

"I guess so," Travis said modestly.

"You must be so proud of Travis," Sara said. "It's been hard for me, coming here and not knowing anybody. Travis has been so good to me. He's the nicest guy I've ever met." She stopped and looked at Travis's parents. "I'm sorry—I'm probably scaring you, aren't I."

"Scaring us?" his father said. "How do you mean?"

"You're probably afraid Travis and I might end up getting married someday."

"Why would that scare us?"

"Because . . . because . . . of what happened to me, but you don't have to worry, because I don't think I'll ever be any good for anyone. I mean to get married—I mean as a wife."

Travis's mother leaned over and patted Sara's arm.

"I don't know why I'm saying these things," Sara said. "I just want you to know you don't need to worry. I'm pretty messed up right now. I see a psychologist twice a week. I tell him things I've never told anyone before. He says it's like opening doors filled with garbage. Well, I've got a lot of closed doors. I'm sorry. I just wanted to tell you not to worry about Travis and me."

It was an awkward situation. Travis's mother bailed them out. "Sara, would you like to come help me dish out the dessert?"

Sara nodded, and the two left the room.

Travis and his father sat there in an awkward silence.

"She's a lovely girl," Travis's father said.

"I know."

"I think I might've ridden a bicycle to Ogden when I was your age for a girl like that."

It surprised Travis that his father could be so human. He smiled.

But his father couldn't leave it at that, because he was worried. "Travis, it's fine to try to help her, but be careful. You have a mission and a temple marriage ahead of you. Don't let anything stand in the way of that."

"I won't."

"Good. See that you don't."

In the kitchen the two women worked on the dessert.

"The Church is very important to you and your family, isn't it," Sara commented.

"Yes."

"I want a family someday, more than anything. But I'm not sure it's possible for me. It's funny, isn't it, how sometimes the things you want the most in life are the things you can't have."

"Sara, I really think you should become a member of the Church."

"Why?"

She put her arm around Sara. "So you'd know just how much God loves you." The dessert was all dished out. "Well, let's go see how it tastes, shall we?"

After supper Travis walked Sara home. They went in her backyard and sat in the lawn chairs.

"I like your parents," she said.

"They like you too."

"I got so nervous beforehand. I'm not sure why. I wanted to make a good impression. I made this dress. It's the last one I'll make that isn't a maternity dress. You may not like me very much when I look like a cow."

He took her hand in his. "It won't matter."

"Oh, Travis, I feel so good when I'm with you." She wanted to lean over and kiss him on the cheek. She was surprised she felt that way. She would have to talk about it with Vernon Collins someday.


THAT EVENING before going to bed, Travis's parents talked. "What do you make of her?" Howard asked.

"I can see why Travis likes her. Can't you?"

"Yes, but I'm not sure I want Travis spending so much time with her."

"Why not?"

"Because she might drag him down."

"Have you ever considered that he might lift her up?"

"Why are you taking her side?" he asked.

"I'm not taking her side. I just keep thinking what I would've been like if I'd been raised in her family."

"But you weren't raised that way."

"Yes, I was one of the lucky ones. But what if I hadn't been? Would I have been so much different from Sara?"

"She's not a member of the Church."

"She will be though, someday."

"You don't know that for sure."

"And you don't know she won't either, do you?" she said.

"If they keep going the way they are, Sara might end up Travis's wife, a nonmember, with Travis having never served a mission. Is that what you want?"

"The boy's not sixteen years old yet. He doesn't even have a driver's license. Isn't it a little early to worry about who he's going to marry?"

"Maybe so," Howard said, "but I want Travis to get more involved with his own age group in our ward. Will you encourage him to do that?"

"Yes, but don't ask me to tell him not to be a friend to Sara. I know there are risks, but I think sometimes we have to reach out to others. Otherwise how'll they ever learn about the gospel?"

"How can you sleep at night with this hanging over our heads?" he asked.

"Howard, we've raised four other boys. At one point, when each one got to be a teenager, we got to where we wouldn't have given a plugged nickel for any of them. And yet they've all turned out okay. Travis has always been a good boy. Sometimes we just have to trust our children to make the right choice."

"And if they don't?"

"Then they learn things the hard way."

They knelt at the side of their bed and prayed for all their sons, but especially for Travis.


THE NEXT DAY Sara met with Vernon Collins.

"Sara, today can we talk about this guilt you're carrying? We keep going over this. Each time we go so far and then you stop me. Can we get beyond your stopping place? You say you feel guilty, and yet we've gone through it time and time again that it was Dillon's fault. No child can ever be held at fault for sexual contact with an adult, no matter how attractive the child is."

"All right, in the beginning it was his fault, but later, when I got older, near the last, it was my fault too."

"How was it your fault when you got older?"

She covered her face with her hands. The psychologist waited.

Finally she said it. "I didn't always fight Dillon."

"But you never invited him, did you?"

"No."

"Then how was it your fault when you got older?"

It was agony to have to say it, but she knew it had to come out. "Sometimes I liked what he did to me. It felt good and I didn't want him to stop."

"And that's why you feel guilty?"

"Yes. I know it was wrong of me to like what he did to me. Don't you see? He got me to have a dirty mind just like him. And now I'm bad and awful and horrible and rotten and dirty—" She started crying. It was the one thing she had kept back because it was too awful to admit, the one secret she thought she would never be able to tell anyone.

"Sara, listen to me. You're not a bad person. Our bodies are designed so that certain things that happen to us feel good. Your body was just reacting. It doesn't matter if it felt good or not, you were still a victim of sexual abuse. He used you, Sara. It's not your fault. Please, Sara, believe me, it's not your fault. He used you. He knew what he was doing. He seduced you. He planned it all out. It was wrong of him to use you. He was the one at fault. It's not your fault, Sara. Please believe me."

She wept, and it was a release, and she knew that another closet in her mind had finally been opened. But there were so many.

Vernon Collins, in spite of all his professional training to be objective and professional, felt his anger swelling up for the man who had done this terrible thing to Sara Corwin.

# Chapter Nine

Kathy was spending another miserable evening in her room. There was a knock on the door. "Who is it?"

"It's me," her mother answered. "Can I come in?"

"I guess so."

Her mother came in and sat down on the bed. "You hardly ate a thing for supper."

"I'm not hungry."

"Is something bothering you?"

"No, just leave me alone."

"Is it about Travis?"

"Yes."

"What's wrong?"

"He's found someone else."

"Who?"

"Her name is Sara. She's staying next door to Travis with the Townsends. He rode his ten-speed all the way to Ogden to get her dog, so he must like her a lot."

"Maybe he just did her a favor."

"Oh, Mother," Kathy grumbled.

"Kathy, I think it's time for you to get contact lenses. I'll kick in whatever your savings won't cover. Also, I think we should have a party."

The next Saturday the young people in the ward got together for a barbecue at Kathy's home. Travis's parents urged him to go, and so he did.

At the party the boys stayed in one group while the girls clustered in another, with only one or two of the more adventurous couples being daring enough to sit together. Travis sat with the guys. He had become somewhat of a celebrity because of Alan's telling everybody about his nearly being the object of a search-and-rescue effort by the police.

"Why did you go all the way to Ogden?" a boy asked.

"The girl staying with our neighbors wanted to get her dog."

"Her name is Sara," Alan said. "I hid in the backyard one morning and saw her come out to talk to Travis. She's a fox."

"You should have brought her with you tonight," another boy said.

"She's kind of bashful."

After his third can of root beer, Travis went to ask Kathy's mother if he could use their bathroom.

"Of course. Do you know where it's at?"

"I'm sure I can find it."

A few minutes later, as he left the bathroom, he noticed Kathy standing in the hallway. He thought she was waiting to use the bathroom. "You must've had a lot of root beer too, right?" he joked.

"One can is all." She said it strangely, much more seriously than he would have thought necessary, considering the subject matter.

"Well, I got you beat. I had three." He started to leave but she was blocking his way. It was an awkward situation. "You're next, I guess."

But Kathy didn't move. "Travis, are you going with Sara?"

"No. We're just friends."

"How come nobody else knows about her?"

"She likes to be alone."

"Why?"

"She just does."

She scowled at him. "You didn't even notice, did you?"

"Notice what?"

"That I got contact lenses."

"Oh, sure. Actually I thought maybe you'd broken your glasses."

"You could've said something. I used all my savings to get them, and you didn't even notice."

He looked into her eyes. "I can't see them. Oh, wait, now I can. Blink once for me, okay?"

He was standing close, staring into her eyes. She was angry at herself for getting weak in the knees when it didn't mean anything except that he wanted to see what happened to her contacts when she blinked.

"You know what, Kathy, you've got nice eyes."

She was still angry, but she couldn't very well start arguing with him after he'd given her a compliment. She decided to just come out and say what was on her mind. "Travis, when do you turn sixteen?"

"September eighteenth."

"My birthday's a week later. I can start dating then, if anybody asks, that is." She scowled. "Probably nobody will though."

"Oh, sure, Kathy, there'll be lots of guys who'll ask you out."

"Who?"

"Gosh, I don't know, lots of guys."

"Will you date when you're sixteen?" she asked, wishing she didn't have to be so pushy. But if she waited for him to act, it would take forever.

"I suppose."

She stepped forward. "Maybe we could go out on a date, Travis, after I turn sixteen."

Travis felt embarrassed for her. He liked her okay, but he didn't appreciate being pushed into taking her out. Besides, she looked so tense and nervous.

"Sure, sometime we'll have to do that," he said. "Well, I gotta go back. See you later."

For the rest of the evening he stayed with the guys, but every once in a while he had to get up to get some more food. Kathy reminded him of a coyote waiting for a sheep to wander out of the flock. Whenever he got up, she'd come and stand next to him.

He felt really sorry for Kathy.

# Chapter Ten

IN AUGUST Travis's family took a vacation. They were gone ten days. When they returned—in fact, as soon as their car pulled into the driveway—Travis ran over to see Sara.

Much had happened in that time. There had been a preliminary hearing in Ogden. Joan and Sara had gone. With Dillon and his wife sitting there, acting as if Sara was making up the whole thing, Sara told the judge what Dillon had done to her. The result of the hearing was that the judge determined there was enough evidence to merit a jury trial.

Also in that time, Sara had begun to wear maternity blouses. She was very sensitive about her changing appearance, and apprehensive about how Travis would accept it. The two of them wandered over to his backyard, where they could be away from Joan's kids. He started picking some vegetables.

"The doctor says I'm very healthy," she said.

"Good."

"He says if I take walks every day, it'll make the delivery go easier." She paused. "While you've been gone, I've been taking walks. I take Muffin with me. Most of the time I wait till it's dark."

"Why do you wait till then?"

She paused. "So nobody will see me."

He stood up. "Let's go for a walk now."

"Together?"

"Of course."

"Not now," she said.

"Why not?"

"Some of your friends might see you with me."

"What if they do?"

"It might start talk."

"I don't care. What counts is the truth, not what people think."

"I still think it'd be better if we waited till after supper."

"All right."

"I go to the doctor once a week now. It's so strange. All these women sitting around the doctor's office, giving their little complaints to each other, but all the time you know they really love it. They're all married and older than me. And then when I get to the dressing room, they ask me to change into this ugly gray robe with slits up the sides, and I sit there for a long time. Then finally the doctor comes and checks me over. I wish they'd have a woman doctor. It's really embarrassing."

His father came outside wearing his gardening clothes. Travis was holding Sara's hand. She pulled away, but Travis wouldn't let go. He wanted his father to see him holding her hand.

"Hello, Sara, how are you doing?"

"Fine. How was your vacation?"

He smiled. "Too short, like always."

"Sure."

"You're beginning to look more like a prospective mother these days."

She blushed. "Joan says that the way I'm getting is beginning to make her look slim. She says she's all for it."

"You look lovely."

"Thank you."

"Travis," his father said, changing the subject, "I was talking to my secretary. We've got quite a backlog of orders for CATTLE-1. I was wondering if you'd like to work for me the next few days."

"Doing what?"

"Mailing out orders. It pays well."

"I guess so."

His father turned to inspect the garden. "It looks like we've got a jungle here now, doesn't it?"

"I'd better get back," Sara said. "Joan asked me to fix supper today."

"When are we going to take that walk?" Travis asked.

"Are you sure you want to go with me?"

"Yes."

"How about nine o'clock?"

"Great."

"Thanks, Travis. It's better not to walk alone."

When he went to get Sara for their walk, she was still getting ready. Joan invited him in.

"How was the preliminary hearing?" Travis asked.

"It was rough," Joan said. "I don't know how Sara got through it."

"Why doesn't her mother just admit what happened?"

"How can she tell a judge she knew her husband was sexually abusing her daughter and yet she did nothing to stop it?"

"It's not fair," Travis said.

"At least she's got us. I'm glad you're not afraid to be her friend."


HIS FATHER WOKE HIM UP at half past five the next morning. After Travis washed up, he went into the kitchen. His father was dishing himself out a large portion of hot whole-wheat cereal. He ate it every morning without even putting sugar on it.

"I cooked extra," he said, about to give Travis some too.

"No thanks. I'll just have some toast and milk."

They ate in silence. His father read in the scriptures a few minutes each day. Travis noticed that he was wearing his gray suit. It used to be his stake conference suit, but when it got too worn it became his campus suit.

Travis turned on the small portable TV on the kitchen table and flipped the channel, trying to find something good. Finally he found cartoons. His father glanced up from the Book of Mormon and saw that Travis was watching cartoons but didn't say anything about it.

Travis finished eating, then went back to his room, waiting for his father to finish his morning routine.

A few minutes later they drove toward campus. "I finished the Book of Mormon today. I spend just five or ten minutes a day, but in a year's time it really builds up."

"I suppose," Travis said.

When they reached the office, Travis realized the only other people in the building were the custodians. They all seemed to know his father quite well. Travis was relieved to know that he was the only professor on campus crazy enough to go to work at six in the morning.

The work was easy enough to do. He took the order form, checked to find out what kind of computer the software would be used on, chose the version of CATTLE-1 for that computer, placed it in a mailing carton, then dumped everything on the desk of a secretary, who typed the mailing label and sealed it up.

Travis ran out of work at eleven that morning. His father asked him if he'd like to go play racquetball with him. Travis couldn't see why his father thought it would be such a treat for Travis to be humiliated in racquetball by his father, who'd won several tournaments over the years. Travis said he'd probably better get back home to take care of his jobs around the yard.

"Maybe some other time then," his father said.

"Sure, Dad, some other time."

Travis asked for a ride home but his father said, "It's less than two miles. You'll enjoy the walk."

Travis didn't know if he'd ever completely understand his father.

# Chapter Eleven

KATHY HAD NEARLY MISSED TRAVIS. It was only because her cat wanted out that she'd seen him walking by the house. She noticed the time: 11:30 A.M. The next day he passed at 12:10.

On the third day she surprised her mother by announcing she was going to weed the flower patch in front of the house. She weeded very slowly. At a little before noon, she looked up and saw Travis coming down the street toward her. She stood up. "Hi, Travis."

"Hi there. Looks like you're working hard."

"Sure. My mother said she'd throw me out of the house if I didn't get it done today. What brings you around here?"

"I've got a job working for my dad on campus. He refuses to give me a ride home. Says the walk'll do me good. I think the real reason is he just wants to save gas money."

She came closer, trying to look her very best.

He smiled and backed away. "Well, I guess I'd better be going. See you later."

Sadly Kathy watched him leave. *I should have asked him in for some lemonade,* she thought, *but maybe he would have thought that's dumb. Besides, I don't even know if we have any lemonade. We have Kool-Aid, but maybe he'd think it's retarded to drink a little kid's drink. What'll I do tomorrow? He's going to think it's strange if I'm weeding the same tiny patch of weeds every morning. He likes red hair. If only my hair were longer.*

She went in to change her clothes.

"Aren't you going to finish weeding?" her mother asked.

"Later." She went to the refrigerator. "Why don't we ever have any lemonade?"

"I didn't even know you wanted some."

"Can you get some today?"

"Well, all right. I'm going shopping anyway."

Kathy spent the afternoon in her room thinking about Travis. She knew he had no idea how much she liked him, but she was afraid that if she told him, it would scare him away.

The next morning at eleven o'clock she began to mow the lawn. She was wearing her swimming suit. It was uncomfortable because the grass was wet and the lawn clippings kept sticking to her legs. But her patience was rewarded when she saw Travis coming. She turned off the mower.

"Hi, Travis," she called out, trying to look alluring while at the same time brushing lawn clippings off her legs.

"Hi, Kathy."

"I'm just about to go in and have a big ice-cold glass of lemonade," she said. "Would you like some too?"

"No thanks. I've got some at home waiting for me. Thanks anyway though." He kept walking.

Kathy stormed into the house. "I want a new swimming suit!"

"What are you talking about?" her mother asked.

"Don't try to talk me out of it. I've got the money for it, and I'm going to buy me a new one today. I might even get a bikini."

"Kathy, you know our standards."

"I've got to have a new swimming suit."

"There's nothing wrong with the one you've got, is there?"

"It's my money, and I should be able to do with it what I want!"

"Kathy, you're not buying a bikini."

Kathy was nearly screaming. "You don't even care what happens to me, do you!" She stormed into her room and slammed the door.

A few minutes later her mother came into Kathy's room. Kathy was sprawled out across the bed. She'd been crying. Her mother sat down on the bed beside her. "Let's talk. Why do you want a new swimming suit?"

"So Travis'll notice me."

"Is that how you want him to notice you, because you're showing off your body?"

"I've got to do *something*. The way it is now, Travis just ignores me, no matter what I say or do. It's like I'm not even there. Sara's so beautiful, I don't have a chance."

That night as Kathy walked around the lawn trying to find another project for the next day, she glanced down the street and saw two people coming down the sidewalk toward her. As they got closer, she realized it was Travis and Sara. She could hear Sara talking. " . . . exercises that'll help when I have my baby . . ."

Kathy thought she'd misunderstood, but then she noticed the loose-fitting blouse Sara was wearing, and suddenly it hit her that Sara was pregnant.

She ran inside and phoned Alan. "What do you know about Sara?"

"Just that she's Travis's girlfriend."

"Did you know she's pregnant?"

"Is that so?" Alan said, sounding strangely happy.

"Yes. I just saw him and Sara walking by here. She's definitely pregnant. There must be an explanation."

Alan snickered. "Oh yeah, sure, there's an explanation all right."

"Alan, I don't think we should say anything until we know the complete story."

"I think I know what the complete story is. Poor Travis. A papa at sixteen." He started laughing again.

Kathy realized she never should have talked to Alan. No matter how much she urged him to keep it quiet, she knew that as soon as she hung up, Alan was going to start telling everybody about Travis and Sara.

After the phone call, she stayed in her room and thought. She was sure there must be another explanation for what she'd seen. Finally she decided to phone Travis and ask him.

When she reached him by phone, she came right to the point. "Is Sara pregnant?"

"Yes. But it wasn't her fault. Her stepdad got her pregnant before she came to live here. It's not her fault."

"I saw you two taking a walk tonight. I didn't know what to think." She paused. "So I phoned Alan and talked to him."

"Oh, no! You told Alan?"

"Yes. I'm sorry. I'll phone him back and see if I can get him to be quiet about it."

"Lots of luck."

"Well, I guess I'd better go now."

"Wait. Sara could use a friend like you. Would you go over tomorrow and talk with her?"

"I wouldn't know what to say."

"Just talk to her. Please, for me."

Kathy couldn't say no to Travis. "All right, I guess so."

THE NEXT DAY Kathy rang Joan's doorbell. Joan came to the door. "Hi, Kathy."

"Travis said this'd be a good time."

"Sara, Kathy's here to see you," she called out.

Kathy went inside just as Sara entered the room.

They sat in the living room, sipping ice-cold soda and eating slices of cantaloupe.

"How do you like it here in Logan?" Kathy asked.

"It's fine."

"Have you been swimming yet?"

"No, I didn't think I should." She paused. "Because of . . . the way I am."

"I've seen women go swimming when they were . . . like you."

"I'm afraid people would make fun."

"I guess I'd feel the same way, if it were me. What will you do about school?"

"I'll be doing some home study. And then after the baby is born, I'll go to high school. That'll be in January."

"Oh."

"There'll be a trial sometime this winter."

"What for?"

"I'm bringing charges against my stepfather. He's the one who got me pregnant. He might end up going to jail. My mother says I'm breaking up the family, but I think he broke up the family the first time he touched me. I stay awake nights worrying about it. Do you think you'd press charges if your father . . ." She noticed Kathy's look of revulsion. "I'm sorry. It's been so long since I've talked to a girl my age. I guess I don't know what to say. I used to have a friend named Diane. The thing I remember the most is the slumber parties we used to have at her house. The whole living room'd be full of girls. We'd sit around all night and eat chips and watch TV and talk. I miss not having a friend like her."

"I guess that's why Travis asked me to come over."

"I guess so. You like Travis, don't you," Sara said.

"Yes, but he doesn't even notice me. I mean, compared to you, I'm nothing."

"That's not true. You've got a lot going for you."

"Like what?"

"It's like when I'm around Travis. I can tell you're good."

"It's the way I was brought up," Kathy said.

"You're lucky to have good parents. Why do you think that happened?"

"Maybe because of what happened in the preexistence."

"The preexistence? What's that?"

"Before we were born, we lived with God."

"What does that have to do with who your parents are?"

"Well, the more righteous were chosen to be born into homes where their parents would be good members of the Church."

Sara looked as if she'd been struck in the face. At first Kathy didn't understand why. "Did I say something wrong?"

"Does that mean I was bad in the preexistence to have been born into a family where my stepfather would abuse me?"

Kathy felt awful. "Well, no . . . it doesn't mean that. I'm sorry. I wasn't thinking. I didn't mean it like that . . . I'm sorry . . . Oh, I knew this would be a mistake. I just don't know what to say to you. What your stepfather did to you is so wrong. It makes me sick to even think about it. Look, I think I'd better go before I say something else that'll hurt you. I'm so sorry. I've got to go now. Thank you for the refreshments."

Kathy hurried home and went in her room and closed the door and wouldn't come out.

# Chapter Twelve

THE NEXT AFTERNOON Sara met with Vernon Collins.

"Yesterday Kathy—she's a friend of Travis's—came over to see me," she told him.

"How did it go?"

"Not very well."

"Why not?"

"I scared her away."

"How did you do that?"

"I told her too much. She couldn't handle it. And then she said something that hurt me, and that made her feel bad, and so she left."

"What did she say?"

"That I must have been bad in the preexistence to have got Dillon as my stepfather."

"Do you believe that?"

"I don't know."

"Do you think God wanted you to be sexually abused?"

"No."

"Neither do I. I think God loves you as much as anyone."

"That's what Joan's always saying. She's getting me to read the Book of Mormon. I might be baptized someday." She paused. "Vernon, are you a Mormon?"

"Yes."

"Joan says that when you're baptized, all your sins are

forgiven. What I want to know is, if I'm baptized, will I be able to forget my past?"

"Probably not."

"That's what I thought too."

"But you can learn to deal with it. That's the most important thing."

"If I live right from now on, could I be married in the temple like Joan and Gary were?"

"Yes."

"But what if I can't be a wife because of what happened to me?"

"Are you worried about that?"

"Yes."

"Sara, you might need counseling at times throughout your life. But you can work through each problem as it comes along. You're a survivor—I have all the confidence in the world in you."

"Thanks, Vernon."


ON THE FIRST DAY OF SCHOOL Travis realized how widespread the rumors about him and Sara were. Some stories maintained that Travis had gotten Sara pregnant, while others dwelt on how weird it was that Travis was going with a girl who was pregnant with someone else's child.

Alan was in his glory because each day he revealed the latest news about the scandal. Sometimes when he ran out of things to say, he made up stories about Sara. Since nobody knew her anyway, and because she was from out of town and, as Alan thought, would probably leave after she had her baby, he didn't see how making up stories about Sara's life before she arrived in Logan could hurt anything.

Sometimes as Travis walked the halls in school, he

overheard guys making fun of him and Sara. A few times he stopped and tried to explain, but it was no use— someone in the group always made everything he said sound dirty. Travis couldn't understand why some people thought anything pertaining to sex had to be treated like it was a big joke. Finally he gave up trying to explain anything. It was hopeless, because whatever he said was met with snickering.

Even though at times it seemed to Travis that the whole school was against him, in truth there were fewer than ten people actively involved in giving him a hard time. But it only took one or two in a hallway, yelling out foul-mouthed comments as he passed, to make him feel that he was walking through enemy territory.

Besides the few who enjoyed making Travis's life miserable, there was a much larger group, made up of the silent majority, who quit even saying hello to Travis when they saw him in the halls. Even those he thought were good friends looked away when they saw him coming. It got to the point where he didn't even want to eat in the school cafeteria, because of the curious stares and crude comments. Eventually he quit eating lunch altogether. Instead he'd go in the library and read.

Travis didn't tell his parents or Sara how things were going at school because he didn't want them to worry.

The highlight of each day was after school, when he stopped by to talk with Sara. And at night Travis and Sara took Muffin for a walk.

One day after school when Travis showed up at Sara's, two sister missionaries were there teaching Sara. He shook hands with them and sat down and waited for them to finish.

After they left, he said, "What's that all about?"

"Just curious." She winced.

"What's wrong?"

"My baby's kicking me. Want to feel it?"

He paused. "I don't think so."

"C'mon, it won't kill you. Come over here."

He sat next to her.

"Put your hand right here."

He gingerly laid his hand on her stomach and felt a light tapping. He turned up his nose. "It's hard to believe there's actually a baby in there. It seems like such a weird way to come into the world. It's so . . . messy."

She smiled. "Oh sure, you'd like it to be done with computers, right?"

"Yeah, that'd be better." He got serious. "Sara, what do you think about the baby that's inside you? Do you hate it?"

"It's not the baby's fault what happened. There's only one person I'm mad at and that's Dillon. But he'll get what's due him at the trial."


AS TRAVIS'S SIXTEENTH BIRTHDAY approached, his mother came up with the idea of having a party. Travis tried to talk her out of it because of what had been happening in school, but she persisted until finally he reluctantly went along with the idea. They came up with a list of fifteen friends to invite. His father used his computer to make up the invitations.

The party was scheduled for seven o'clock the Saturday evening following his birthday.

On the day of the party, Travis took a long hike in the morning. When he got home, about two in the afternoon, he felt guilty as he realized his mother had been working all day in preparation for the party. "You shouldn't go to all this trouble," he said.

"It's no trouble. Besides, you only turn sixteen once

in your life, you know. Now, let me see, what games do you and your friends want to play?"

"I don't think there'll be that many coming."

"Oh, don't be silly. If you invite fifteen, there'll be at least ten or so who'll show up. Are there some games you'd like to play?"

"No."

"How about if we set up the Ping-Pong table in the garage?"

"The hinge came off a couple of years ago and we never got it fixed."

"Your father isn't doing much now. I'm sure he can get it fixed in time."

"He doesn't have to do that."

"He'd be happy to do it for you." She called out, "Howard . . ."

A few minutes later Travis went to his room and closed the door. He could hear his father using the electric drill to fix the Ping-Pong table and his mother in the kitchen mixing up a second cake. She'd already made one cake but then decided it wouldn't be enough. He tried to convince her that one cake would be enough, but she wouldn't believe him.

Travis sat down on his bed. He felt awful. His parents were going to all this work for him because they didn't know yet that he didn't have any friends anymore. He knelt down and said a prayer and then returned to the kitchen. His mother was busily working away. A strand of her hair had slipped down onto her forehead. He reached over and lovingly brushed it into place. "Mom, this is way too much cake."

"Nonsense. I've raised enough kids to know how much a bunch of teenagers can eat."

"What can I do to help?"

"Not a thing. This is your special day—just relax and enjoy it. After your dad is finished with the Ping-Pong table, I'll have him help me string some crepe paper in the living room and that'll pretty much do it. You go take your shower and get ready."

Travis wandered out into the garage. His father was still working on the Ping-Pong table.

"Need any help, Dad?"

"No thanks, I've just about got it done. I put extra braces on the legs so the table'll be a little more sturdy."

Travis was aware how much time it had taken his father to fix the table. "Shouldn't you be getting ready for your classes on Monday?"

"This is more important. We want you and your friends to have a nice time tonight."

"Maybe not everyone we invited will be coming."

"It doesn't matter. Whoever comes will have a nice time." He finished what he was doing. "Well, how's that? Try wiggling the table."

Travis tried the table. "It's great, Dad."

"Should have done it ages ago. Let's see, do you happen to know where the paddles and balls are?"

"No."

His father looked at his watch. "Well, no matter. I still have time to go down and buy some."

"You don't need to do that. The old ones are around here somewhere."

"We don't have time to find them. Besides, they're not that expensive. I'll just run down and get some." He started to leave.

"Dad," Travis called out, his voice faltering, "I don't think we're going to need any paddles."

"Why not?"

"There might not be that many who come."

"Don't be such a pessimist. It only takes two to play

Ping-Pong, and I'm sure there'll be at least that many. You go get ready. I'll run down to the store. I'll be right back."

The party was scheduled at seven. At six thirty Sara came over and asked if she could help. She was given the job of doing the crepe paper and the balloons.

At six forty-five his father came in the house. "Well, we're all set for Ping-Pong."

At five minutes to seven, Kathy came over. She nodded at Sara and sat down next to Travis.

At seven o'clock all the last-minute arrangements were finished.

At ten minutes after seven, Jim Simons, a friend from school, showed up. Jim and Travis sat next to each other in math. Jim had heard rumors about Travis, but he didn't believe them. Besides, he wasn't in the select group of Travis's friends who'd all agreed not to go to the party.

At twenty minutes after seven they were still sitting around, glancing at the clock, waiting for other guests to arrive.

"I bet I put the ice cream in the punch too soon," his mother said. "It'll all be melted. Travis, are you sure you said seven o'clock on the invitations?"

"Yes."

"But people are always confusing those two times," his father said. "I bet everyone's thinking it's at seven thirty."

"I think I'll put the punch in the freezer," his mother said. She got up and began ladling the thick drink from the punch bowl into pitchers.

"That really looks good," Kathy said.

"Oh, it is. Here, take a taste." She poured out a small sample for everyone. They each took a taste and said how good it tasted.

"It takes a while to prepare, but I think it's worth it. I got the recipe in Relief Society from a woman who used to be the dessert chef at a fancy hotel in San Francisco."

"Anybody want to play Ping-Pong?" his father asked.

"I'll play you, Travis," Jim said.

"How about later," Travis said.

"Oh, later there'll be a line," his father said. "Now's the time to play before the crowd gets here."

Travis's head felt like he was on fire. He excused himself and went in the bathroom and splashed his face with cold water. He wished he could stay in there all night. He dreaded having to go out and watch his mother fuss over refreshments that weren't even needed.

When he returned, his mother cleared her throat the way she did when things were tense. "Travis, are you sure you mailed out all the invitations?"

"I was the one who mailed them," his father responded.

"Oh." His mother sounded almost disappointed to have lost a possible explanation why nobody else had shown up yet.

They continued to wait, but there were no steps up the walk, no cars coming to a stop in their driveway, no noise of people approaching the house.

Kathy knew nobody else was coming. She'd heard people talking in school.

"Well," Travis's mother said, "let's wait a few more minutes, and then I'll get the punch from the freezer. I can't leave it in there too long or the whole thing'll freeze." Her voice began to falter. "I just don't understand . . . fifteen invitations . . . and three people show up."

"I can't stand this," Kathy said, suddenly standing up. "Sister Fitzgerald, nobody else is coming because of the things people at school are saying about Travis."

"What do you mean?" his mother asked.

"Sara, don't you know you're ruining Travis's life? He doesn't have any friends anymore because of you."

"That's not true," Travis said quickly.

"Oh, Travis, you know it is. Everybody's talking about you two. You think Alan's your friend? Well, he's the worst of all. People are saying such ugly things about you and Sara. I keep telling them the stories aren't true, but nobody believes me. Travis, nobody can understand why you're spending time with a pregnant girl. The main reason why people didn't come tonight is because they knew Sara'd be here."

Kathy turned to Sara. "I'm sorry if it sounds like I don't like you, but I've known Travis a long time, and it's really hard for me to see him being hurt. I'm sorry, but I can't stay here any longer. Happy birthday, Travis." She ran out the door.

They sat there stunned.

Travis's mother got to her feet. Still in shock, she stammered, "I'd better go get the punch before it freezes, and then I think maybe we'd better serve it. Is it all right with everyone if I don't put it in the punch bowl? We probably don't need a punch bowl for just three guests." She rushed into the kitchen. They could hear her burst into tears. Travis's father hurried out to comfort her.

Sara stood up. Tears were streaming down her face. "I'm so sorry, Travis. I didn't know how it was for you. I've got to go home now."

He grabbed her hand. "Don't go. Please, I need you here with me. Please, Sara. My mother worked so hard, all day—and we have two big cakes and all that punch and nobody to eat it. Please stay. Don't leave me here all alone. I need you, please, stay with me."

Sara sat down and waited for the refreshments to be over with.

They could hear Travis's mother crying and his
father talking to her to help her get control of her feelings again. Travis tried to wipe away his own tears in
such a way that Jim and Sara wouldn't notice. Then he
looked over at Sara. She was crying too.

He looked at Jim. He was self-consciously staring at a
napkin, folding it over and over again into ever smaller
shapes.

"Most of the time my birthday parties aren't like
this."

Jim nodded. "That's good."

Suddenly, seeing this from Jim's point of view, Travis
started laughing. And then Sara did too.

Travis decided to change the mood of the party. He
went to the piano and played a song and got Sara and
Jim to sing along.

A few minutes later his parents returned, both of
them doing their best to look happy. "Well, I guess it's
time," his mother began, "to wish Travis a happy . . ."
She waited for the grief to pass. ". . . a happy birthday.
Let's all sing 'Happy Birthday to Travis.'"

Then they had cake and punch. Travis talked Sara
into staying long enough to watch him and Jim play
Ping-Pong.

After the party, Travis said, "Dad, the table was just
great. I'll never forget how you fixed it for me for my
birthday."

"Should've done it years ago," his father said, his
voice husky with emotion, as he began to understand the
ordeal Travis was going through.


AFTER THAT Kathy cut herself off from any contact
with Travis. She didn't bother anymore to defend him in
school when people said cruel things about him. And

when she had her sixteenth birthday party, she didn't invite him.

At the next stake conference Travis's father spent fifteen minutes talking about the dangers of backbiting and spreading gossip. But it didn't help much, because even as he spoke, Alan sat in the back of the congregation with his friends, whispering something very sensational, although completely untrue, about Sara's life before she'd come to town.

# Chapter Thirteen

ALL THROUGH OCTOBER the sister missionaries—Sister Rafael from San Bernardino, California, and Sister Amundson from Athens, Ohio—continued to teach Sara the gospel. It would have been difficult for Sara to explain, even to Vernon Collins, how she felt about those two. She looked forward to their visits. She wanted to be like them. To her, they were what God wanted a young woman to be. They made her feel important and loved and worthwhile. Their smiles seemed to light up the room. And when they taught, Sara knew somehow that what they said was true.

"What do you think about the things we've been talking about?" Sister Rafael asked her one day.

"I believe what you've told me so far."

"That's great. We'd like you to go to church with us next Sunday."

Sara cleared her throat. "Oh."

"Is there something wrong with that?"

"I'm afraid people'll make fun of me."

"They won't. Besides, we'll be with you all the time. And Joan and Gary and Travis—all of us will be there with you."

Sara couldn't refuse Sister Rafael, and so next Sunday she went to church. Just as they'd assured her, during sacrament meeting she was surrounded by her friends—Travis on the left and Sister Rafael and her companion to her right, and then Joan and Gary and their children.

Before the service began, Sara leaned over and asked Travis if Alan was there at church today. She was curious because he was the one Kathy had said was telling lies about her.

Travis started blushing. "Yes, he's here."

"Where is he?"

Travis sheepishly pointed to one of the two boys sitting at the sacrament table.

She turned to Sister Rafael, sitting on her other side. "Those two guys. Why are they sitting there?"

"They'll bless the sacrament. It's like they're standing in for the Savior. They'll be saying the same prayer he said for his apostles at the Last Supper."

The fact that Alan was at church, about to represent the Savior, but the rest of the week went around telling lies about her—that was very hard for Sara to understand.

To make matters worse, during the opening song Kathy looked back and scowled at her.

After sacrament meeting, Sara went to the restroom. When she entered, she found a group of girls, twelve or thirteen years old, fussing over their hair.

One of them, noticing how young Sara was to be pregnant, asked, "Are you married?"

"No."

The girl got a cruel smile on her face. "Well, I guess we all know what you've been doing, don't we?" The other girls started giggling.

Sara immediately left the restroom and found Sister Rafael. "I'm going home now."

"Is anything the matter?"

"No, I just have to go home, that's all. It's not far. I can walk. Tell Joan for me, okay?"

When she got home to the empty house, she went in the kitchen to make sure the roast in the oven was okay, and then decided to surprise Joan and make a Jell-O salad for their Sunday meal.

Sara felt hurt and angry. It didn't make sense. The things Sister Rafael and Sister Amundson taught seemed so good, and yet those girls in the restroom, members of the Church, had been so rude. And Alan, the one she felt was the furthest away from being Christ-like, was the one asked to represent Jesus in blessing the sacrament. *How can the Church be true if things like this are going on?* she thought.

She knew she had reason enough not to get baptized.

But then she thought about Joan and Gary and Travis and his parents and Sister Rafael and Sister Amundson. They made God an important part of their lives.

*Maybe not everybody in the Church lives the way they should,* she thought, *but maybe God's willing to take us where we are and work with us. That wouldn't be too bad,* she decided, *if that means he's willing to take me the way I am now.*

She finished preparing the salad and went to her room. She was all alone in an empty house. It seemed like a good time to pray. She felt so big and clumsy. It was such a chore to kneel down beside her bed. But she did it anyway.

"Father in heaven . . ."

She stopped. She felt a great calm, peaceful feeling, like a fresh breeze across her soul, and somehow she knew that God was her Father in heaven, that he loved her, and that what she'd been through grieved him. She felt strongly that the child she'd soon give birth to was also loved by God, and that her baby would be well cared for by its adoptive parents. She felt certain that the gospel of Jesus Christ was true. The gospel net was big

enough to accept all who would come to it. She didn't
have to worry about how well other people lived the gospel; all she had to do was to live the way she should. She
understood, now more than ever before, that God had so
loved the world that he gave his Only Begotten Son, that
whosoever believes in him should not perish, but have
everlasting life.

She was Sara, beloved of God.

When Joan and Gary came home, they could tell
she'd been crying.

"Is anything wrong?" Joan asked.

"No, everything is wonderful. I've decided to be baptized right away."


"I'M GOING TO BE BAPTIZED on Saturday," she told Vernon at their next session. "Will you come?"

"Yes, of course. I'd be delighted."

"I'm going to live my life for God from now on."

"That sounds good. What do you want to do with the
life God has given you?"

"I want to help other girls who've been abused."

"Good. What else?"

"I want to get married in the temple and be like Joan.
She's the greatest."

"You never mention Joan's husband. Why's that?"

"Oh, he's nice too."

"Does he ever hug you?"

"No."

"Do you want him to?"

"No."

"Why not?"

"It wouldn't be fair to Joan."

"Are you worried you might take him away from
her?"

She thought about it. "I guess so. There's a part of me that still thinks I have powers over men. Maybe that's why I stay away from Gary."

"What would happen if you asked Gary for a hug?"

She shook her head. "I could never do that."

"Why not? Joan'd be in the same room with you. I think it'd be all right with her, don't you? Why don't you try it?"

She paused. "I'll think about it."


TRAVIS, dressed in white baptismal clothes, sat on the first row of chairs, just in front of the baptismal font. He was nervous. Sara would be the first person he'd baptized after being made a priest. He hoped he'd get it right the first time.

Sara came in and sat down. She was wearing the largest baptismal gown they could find. In the dressing room she'd joked with Joan that it made her look like a moving tent.

But to Travis Sara was more beautiful than ever before. There was a radiance in her countenance he'd never seen before. She reached over and grabbed his hand and squeezed it. "You'd better not drown me," she whispered.

Travis's parents were sitting in the second row. Travis knew they were worried about him. Once in a while, out of the blue, they would say something that he could tell they had carefully rehearsed in their minds beforehand. Mostly it was about a mission and temple marriage—how important both things were. His mother had started clipping little messages and putting them on the refrigerator, cutouts from newspapers and magazines, messages from church leaders.

Sister Rafael and Sister Amundson were sitting in the

third row. Vernon Collins came in and sat in the back
row. Sara saw him and went back and brought him up to
sit next to Joan and Gary, and then returned to Travis.
"He's my shrink," she whispered.

"Must be a tough job," he whispered back.

Still maintaining reverence, she poked him in the
ribs. He smiled.

"This is the happiest I've ever been in my life," she
whispered.

"Me too."

The bishop began the service. There was an opening
song, a prayer, a talk by Gary about baptism, and then
they all went to the baptismal font. Travis entered first
and took Sara's hand as she walked down the stairs into
the water.

Travis looked up at his father, who nodded. Then he
took Sara's wrist with his left hand, raised his right hand
to the square, bowed his head, and began the prayer. He
said the words slowly and distinctly, and when he was
through he said amen, put his right hand on the small of
her back, and baptized her.

When Sara came out of the water, she looked
radiant. "This is so wonderful!" she cried out.

Travis helped her up the stairs and then went to the
men's dressing room. He took off his wet clothing, dried
himself off quickly, and began dressing.

His father came in. "You did a good job, Travis."

"Thanks, Dad. I had a good teacher."

"You've set a good example for Sara. You'll always be
important to her, because you were the one who baptized her. That'll be true in the mission field too."

"I know, Dad," Travis said, suspecting that was the
main reason his father had come in to see him.

"Well, I guess I'd better get back and let you finish
getting ready. See you later." He left.

Travis wondered what it must be like to be a father and always be worried. He finished dressing before Sara did and returned to the baptismal room. He sat down and listened to the bishop's wife play some hymns on the piano. A few minutes later Sara returned. Her hair was still damp, but she looked wonderful. Travis had never seen her look as much at peace with herself as she did then.

Gary confirmed her a member of the Church, with the bishop and Vernon Collins and Travis's father standing in.

After the confirmation, Sara stood up, turned to the bishop and shook his hand, shook Vernon Collins's hand, and turned to Gary. Winking at Vernon, she threw her arms around Gary and hugged him. "Thanks, Dad."

Gary smiled. "Hey, you're welcome, daughter."

Sister Rafael and Sister Amundson came up to embrace her too. But Joan gave Sara the biggest and best hug of the evening.

There was a closing song, a prayer offered by Travis's father, and then the two families went to Joan and Gary's for cake and ice cream.


A WEEK LATER there was a youth dance. Travis's parents encouraged Travis to go. He went mainly because he had two people he needed to see.

"Alan, I need to talk to you." They walked to where nobody could overhear them. "Kathy says you're telling lies about Sara."

"What kind of lies?"

Travis told him what he'd heard.

"I'd never do anything like that," Alan said.

"You'd better not, Alan, that's all I can say."

Next he visited with Kathy. "After Sara has her baby

and her father's trial is over, she's going to start school. If you could just be with her, you know, and help her . . ."

"You're hopeless, Travis. Excuse me, I have to go help with the refreshments."

Travis watched her leave. Kathy had been his only hope.

# Chapter Fourteen

TRAVIS'S BROTHERS and their families all came home for Christmas, which meant that Travis was moved out of his room onto the living room couch, and that during the day there were wall-to-wall kids in the house.

Sometimes when Travis walked into the room, he'd notice the adult conversation come to an abrupt and awkward stop. He realized his brothers and their wives and his parents were talking about him and Sara. Every time he turned around, one of his brothers was encouraging him to be sure and go on a mission.

He spent much of the Christmas vacation with Sara. By that time she was so big she didn't want to go out much. On the day before Christmas they played a marathon game of Monopoly. After Christmas he took the video game he'd gotten as a present over to her house and hooked it up, and they played for hours.

For Christmas he gave her a necklace, and she gave him a tie she'd made for him.

THE SIXTH OF JANUARY is a date Travis will never forget. It began to snow in the early afternoon. After school Travis shoveled the sidewalk. Since Joan and Gary's walk wasn't done, he started on it too. When he was about halfway finished, he saw his mother rushing over to Joan's house. "Travis, Sara's gone into labor. I'm going to watch the kids while Joan takes Sara to the hospital."

Travis cleared a path from the front door to Joan's car. As Sara came out, Joan and Travis helped her to the car.

"Travis, this is it," Joan said.

As Sara eased herself into the front seat of the car, Travis saw the pain etched on her face. "Joan, can I go to the hospital with you?" he asked.

"It's up to Sara."

"I don't care."

Joan stepped aside while Travis shut Sara's door. "It's no picnic, Travis, I'll warn you beforehand."

"I know, but I want to be with Sara."

"All right, get in the back."

Joan drove as fast as she dared, considering the heavy snowfall. After what seemed an eternity they pulled into the emergency entrance of the hospital. There was some delay while information was filled out, but finally Sara was admitted.

Travis phoned his mother and told her he was going to stay at the hospital. On his way into the labor room, a nurse stopped him. "Only husbands or immediate family are allowed in here."

He knew he had to get in there. "I'm Sara's brother."

"All right, come in."

Sara was in bed, separated from the other beds by a curtain drawn around it.

Travis was not prepared for this. Each time Sara started gasping with another pain, her breathing fast, fear and suffering on her face, he thought she might die before the pain subsided.

Sara was the only patient in the labor room, and she was far from ready to have a baby, and so for the two nurses on duty it was a slack time. "Did I tell you I joined a bowling league?" one of them said. "It's a Saturday morning league. Last week was my first time. I did rotten, but still it's a lot of fun. Just a bunch of us from the floor. Ellie got me into it."

Another pain came. Sara gasped and squeezed Joan's hand.

The nurse continued. "Guess what I bowled my first game—85. I could've died. But nobody seemed to mind. We're just in it for the fun. It's like the girls' night out, except it's Saturday mornings. I'm sure we're never going to win anything. We got to giggling on one game, and, I'll tell you, you would have thought we were a bunch of schoolgirls. You ought to get in on this. Alice will be leaving the team when her husband graduates, so why don't you come along?" She laughed. "We call ourselves the Bedpans. Isn't that a riot? Marge thought it up."

"Oh! Oh!" Sara cried out.

Travis barged into the nurses' station. "Why don't you do something instead of just standing around?"

"We've given her something to help with the pain. These things take time. Don't worry. She's doing fine. Look, maybe you should wait out in the waiting room."

"No, I'm staying here."

A minute passed and then the first nurse started up again. "The thing is, I never learned how to put any spin on the ball. You're supposed to have it curve in between pins one and three. You get more pin action that way. But not me. Right straight down the alley. So what do I do? Work on the spin and let my score drop? Or just keep doing it the old way?"

"Ooooh!" Sara cried out. Her hands were on her head, the veins on her neck throbbing, her breathing fast and coming in bursts.

Joan was gently wiping Sara's forehead with a cloth.

"It's all right, hon. You're doing great. Just try to relax as much as possible."

A few minutes later a second woman was admitted to the labor room. Travis and Sara didn't see her, but they could hear her and her husband talking to one of the nurses.

"Is this your first one?" the nurse asked.

The woman laughed. "No. It'll be our fifth."

"Then I guess I don't have to tell you what to do then, do I."

"Oh no, we'll manage just fine."

An hour passed, and then two. The other woman in labor was wheeled into the delivery room and had her baby. Sara's pains got worse and closer together. After a while she was crying nearly all the time. And sometimes she screamed. Travis felt as if he couldn't stand it anymore. He escaped to the empty waiting room at the end of the hall and stood at the window and looked out. The snow was still falling. He sat down and rummaged through the stack of magazines on the coffee table.

He began thumbing through a copy of *Sports Illustrated*. He turned to the first article and began reading. It was all about the Boston Celtics. He tried to concentrate on the words . . . Larry Bird's fall-away jump shot . . . She's dying . . . Larry Bird's fall-away jump shot . . . There's nothing I can do . . . Larry Bird's fall-away jump shot . . . What if she dies? . . . Larry Bird's fall-away jump shot made the difference in the game with the Philadelphia Seventy-Sixers . . . If she dies and I've never told her I love her . . . Larry Bird's fall-away jump shot . . . It wasn't her fault, none of it . . . Larry Bird's fall-away jump shot . . . There will never be another girl I'll care about as much as her . . . Larry Bird's fall-away jump shot made the difference in the game with the Philadelphia Seventy-Sixers . . .

He knew he should be with Sara and tell her everything was going to be all right, but he didn't know that for sure, and maybe it wasn't going to be all right—maybe Sara was going to die.

He wanted to run away and hide. He wanted to go home and get into bed and get up in the morning and go to school and have his biggest worry be that his math assignment wasn't done.

She's dying, he thought. She's going to die right in front of me, and there's nothing I can do to stop it. I love her. She doesn't know how much. She's the only thing in my life that matters anymore, and I've never told her. And now she's dying, and if she dies, then I'll die too, because I love her so much.

Tears were streaming down his face, and he couldn't seem to get control of himself. He started to go into the labor room, but then he heard Sara crying, and he couldn't face it anymore. He stumbled out into the hallway again. He saw a pay phone. He found a quarter in his pocket, dropped it in, and dialed home.

His father answered.

Travis was crying hysterically. "Dad, I'm so afraid, I think Sara's dying. Please help me."

"I'll come right over, son."

Travis waited just outside the doorway of the labor room. Sara screamed. He slumped to the floor and put his hands over his ears to keep the sound away. Larry Bird's fall-away jump shot . . . Larry Bird's fall-away jump shot . . . Larry Bird's fall-away jump shot . . . No matter how hard he tried, he couldn't make it go away.

When he finally spotted his father and Gary coming, he ran down the hall and threw his arms around his father. He knew everything would be all right now. It always had been, and it always would be.

His father and Gary gave Sara a priesthood blessing. Travis watched. He realized how much he loved his father. He admired how calmly he did things, how full of faith he was, how much strength there was in him. And then to hear the slow, calm words of the priesthood blessing, and to feel his father's faith and strength . . . He realized that somehow in growing up he'd over-looked his own father, looking for heroes in other places when the greatest hero he'd ever known lived at home.

After the priesthood blessing, Gary excused himself to go back to be with his own kids. Travis and his father went to the deserted waiting room to wait.

"I love her, Dad."

"I know you do."

"What should I do?"

"What do you mean?"

"I've been thinking—maybe I should marry her so she can keep the baby."

"I think the baby would be better off being adopted."

"Sara'd be a good mother."

"Yes, of course, but think about the couple who'll get her baby if she gives him up. No doubt they've waited for years to have a baby. They'll shower that child with love and affection. And they'll have the maturity and the re-sources that a sixteen-year-old married couple can't pos-sibly have."

"But I don't want to lose Sara."

"If you really love her, give her time to grow up. If you marry her now, she'll miss the best part of being a teenager."

Travis paused. "What part is that, Dad?"

His father looked over at him. "It hasn't been that much fun for you lately, has it."

"Not really."

"Things'll get better."

"So you don't think it's a good idea for Sara and me to get married and keep the baby."

"No, I don't, son."

"Maybe you're right. If this night is anything like

what it's like to be a parent, I'm definitely not ready for it."

At two thirty in the morning, Sara was wheeled into the delivery room. His father put his arm around Travis's shoulder as they walked the halls. "You're certainly growing up fast these days. It wasn't until I was twenty-six that I spent the night in a labor room of a hospital."

"Dad, after I got here and saw what it was like, I wished I'd never come."

His father smiled. "You want to know a secret? I felt the same way."

"It was too much for me. I couldn't handle it. I'm glad you came, Dad. I knew I could depend on you."

His father, visibly moved, only nodded. "You can. Always."

At 3:19 in the morning, Sara's baby was born, a girl, six pounds five ounces.


THAT AFTERNOON Travis visited Sara in the hospital. He brought her flowers. "How are you feeling?"

"Tired."

"Me too. I missed school today. My mom let me sleep in. I slept until noon."

"Lazy bum," she said with a weak smile.

"How's your baby?"

"They say she's fine."

"Haven't you seen her yet?" he asked.

"Not yet. They're only going to let me see her once. And then they'll keep her in the nursery for a few days just to be sure she's doing okay. And then, without me knowing about it, the couple who's adopting her will come and get her. So I'll only see my baby one time."

"Do you wish you could keep her?"

"Yes, but I know it's best this way."

TRAVIS AND GARY AND JOAN were with Sara when they brought her baby in. Sara held her for a long time and then let Joan and Gary each hold her. Joan predicted she'd have Sara's eyes and hair, although there wasn't much hair there to be able to tell.

"Travis, would you like to hold her?" Sara asked.

Gingerly he picked her up. He marveled at her tiny fingers.

In the midst of this, a woman from the state adoption agency came into the room.

"Sara, whenever you're ready," she said softly.

The room grew still.

Sara asked for her baby, and Travis, who had been holding her, laid her softly in Sara's arms. She lightly touched the baby's mouth and cheeks, nose and fingers, as if trying to memorize by touch and sight each feature.

"It's so hard to do this," she said.

Joan sat down on the bed and stroked Sara's hair. "I know it is, hon."

"My baby, my little precious baby . . ."

Travis had to turn away.

The woman from the adoption agency knew this was hard for Sara. "Would you like me to come back in a few minutes?"

"No. In a few minutes, I won't let you have her. You'd better take her now."

The woman reached down and gently picked up the baby. "We'll take good care of her."

"Please go," Sara whispered through her tears.

The woman nodded and quickly left the room with the baby.

The next day Travis returned to school. As he walked down the halls, still in a daze, he felt as if he'd come from a different planet.

# Chapter Fifteen

THE TRIAL BEGAN in Ogden ten days after the baby was born. The day before it began, Travis told Sara he would be there with her.

"I don't want you there," she said.

"Why not?"

"It'd be too embarrassing for me." She paused. "Besides, we'll come home every day. Just be here for me to talk to. That's all I need."

"All right, if that's the way you want it."

In many ways he was relieved.

TRAVIS SAT at the dining room table and hurried to finish his homework, looking out the window often to see if Joan and Sara had returned yet. Finally at seven o'clock the car pulled into the driveway. He put on his coat and ran across just as Sara got out of the car. They all went inside.

Gary had fed the kids and put them to bed, but when they heard Sara they all came running out in their pajamas and hugged her.

"Have you eaten?" Gary asked.

"We had something in Ogden, but I'm still hungry. Sara, how about you?"

"Later, maybe. I just want to be with Travis."

They sat together on the couch. "Was it hard?" he asked.

"Yes, very."

"What did they do?"

"First they decided on a jury, and then each lawyer made his opening remarks, and then I started on my testimony."

"What did Dillon do?"

"He glared at me. I think he'd have killed me right there in the courtroom if he thought he could get away with it." She stopped. "Oh, they entered the blood test results too. Look, I don't want to talk about it anymore. Can we just go to a movie?"

"Sure, whatever you want."

It was a good movie, full of action and adventure, just what they needed to escape. They ate popcorn and drank diet soda and tried to forget about tomorrow.


THE SECOND NIGHT, when Sara and Joan got home at nine o'clock, Sara got out of the car, slammed its door as hard as she could, and then stormed into the house, brushing past Travis as if he weren't even there.

"Is it okay if I go in?" Travis asked Joan.

"Sure, but don't be surprised if she bites your head off. She's still fuming. Dillon's lawyer was really rough on her today."

Travis went to Sara's room and knocked. "Sara," he called out.

"Go away! I don't want to talk to you."

"I'm staying here until you come out."

She came out and marched into the kitchen and grabbed a knife.

"What are you doing?"

"I'm going to make a stupid salad! Is there any law against that? I need my stupid vitamins." She opened the refrigerator and pulled out some vegetables, got a gigantic bowl, placed a whole head of lettuce on the chopping block, and whacked the lettuce with the knife over and over. Then she grabbed a handful of carrots and chopped angrily away until they were large, uneven globs of carrot. She dumped everything into the salad bowl and doused the whole thing with salad dressing. And then she took one bite. "I hate salads!"

"Sara," he said.

"What?" she snapped.

"Cool down."

Joan went in to talk to Gary and see how things had gone. He'd taken the day off to watch the kids. The kids, in pajamas, came out to see Sara, but Joan herded them back in their rooms so they'd be out of Sara's way.

Travis reached over to take Sara's hand. She pulled back angrily. "Joan!" she called out. Joan came in. "Tell Travis how I tried to run off with every guy I ever saw. Go ahead, tell him what a dirty tramp I am."

Joan turned to Travis. "That's what Dillon's lawyer tried to prove today."

"And to top it off," Sara growled, "my mother said it was true." She picked up the salad bowl. "Does anybody want any of this slop?"

Joan and Travis shook their heads.

She dumped it all into the garbage can. "Lawyers!" she grumbled. "Dillon's lawyer asks me how I can remember all those details when it's been so long since they happened. If those things had happened to him, I'll guarantee he'd remember every detail. And then they parade all these character witnesses for Dillon. Wow, why doesn't Dillon run for governor? I mean, he's such an outstanding citizen, so active in the community, kind to children, a good father, a pillar of the community. Dillon's lawyer has them all thinking I'm the guilty one. Why does everything always have to work against me?"

Joan tried to explain. "It's Dillon's lawyer's job to get people to believe he's innocent, but it doesn't mean people believe him."

"Travis, you should've been there. Dillon's lawyer wears a three-piece suit. He's got gray hair and a voice that sounds like a Hollywood actor. And what do I get? An assistant district attorney with a plaid sports coat. His glasses keep falling down, and his voice is a joke. I asked how many cases like this he'd prosecuted, and guess what he tells me? This is the first one! So tell me, who do you believe?"

"We believe you," Travis said.

"Well, you're the only ones." She began pacing the floor. "Oh, I feel so rotten, I feel like my head's going to blow up."

"Want to take a walk?" Travis asked.

"Now there's a stupid idea if I ever heard one. But that's just like you, Travis. You always think nature can cure everything, don't you? Well, look outside. For your information it's snowing."

"We'll dress warm."

"You can wear my jogging outfit if you want," Joan said.

Sara paused. "You're both serious, aren't you."

"Yes."

"All right, I'll go. With any luck I'll catch pneumonia and die."

Joan made sure Sara was bundled up well when they left. It was snowing but the wind wasn't blowing. They walked a long time in silence. Finally she talked. "I'm sorry for being such a witch tonight."

"No problem."

"Travis, you're my knight in shining armor, aren't you?"

"I'll be whatever you need me to be."

"If the jury finds Dillon innocent, will you quit being my friend?"

"No way. It'd take more than that to get rid of me. Besides, Dillon's going to be convicted."

"Travis, he's going to get off free. I can tell. I've been looking at the people on the jury. Yesterday they looked me in the eye. Today after Dillon's lawyer finished, they didn't. So the whole thing has been a waste of time. All that it's accomplished is that I've had to be abused one more time by Dillon—this time in front of an audience."

"They can't possibly let Dillon go free."

"You wait and see."

On her doorstep, they stopped to say goodnight. "The case'll go to the jury tomorrow," she said. "If we come home honking the horn, you'll know they found Dillon guilty."

The next night, at three in the morning, Joan and Sara returned home. They pulled quietly into the driveway and went inside. Travis, who'd been trying to stay awake, had fallen asleep just before they arrived. He slept through until the next morning.

The verdict was not guilty.

# Chapter Sixteen

TWO DAYS LATER Sara and Vernon met again. At first Sara was a stone wall, but after a while Vernon was able to get her to talk about it. Once she started, he realized how devastated she'd been by the verdict. There were no tears, only anger. "If Dillon's innocent, then that must mean I'm guilty. So you've wasted all this time on me for nothing."

"I can understand why you're angry about the way the trial turned out."

"Angry? Why should I be angry? Dillon always gets his way. He always has with me, you know. Always."

"Why did Dillon go free?"

"Simple. Because he's innocent."

"Sara, calm down and tell me what the real reason is."

"They say it was a technical point."

"What kind of a technical point?"

"They couldn't accuse him of incest because he isn't my real father, so they chose forcible rape, but they couldn't prove it was by force all the time, because like I've told you, I didn't fight him tooth and nail every time. So Dillon goes free. Makes a lot of sense, right?"

"I talked to a lawyer friend of mine last night. He tells me there's new legislation pending that'll make it much easier to get a conviction on a case like this."

"A lot of good that does me. The worst thing about it for me is to know that my mother told the world I was a tramp. She lied just to save her marriage to that animal. I'll never forgive her for that."

"Never is a long time."

"You tell me why I should ever forgive her."

"For your own peace of mind. In time I hope you'll be able to forgive Dillon too."

"Why am I the one who always has to do the changing?"

"Because you can't change anyone but yourself."

Finally the tears came. "Vernon, I feel so awful. Sometimes I get so tired of even trying."


THE BISHOP INVITED KATHY in to talk with him. "Kathy, I have a special assignment for you."

"What?"

"There's a new member of our ward. Her name is Sara Corwin. She's sixteen. She was baptized recently, and she'll be in the Laurel class. I'd like you to fellowship her."

Kathy frowned. "I guess you know she just had a baby, don't you?"

"Yes, I know that."

"Then why does she have to be in with us girls? I think she should go to Relief Society, so she can be there with all the other mothers."

"She didn't keep the baby. I've talked to the Laurel adviser and we both think it'd be best if she went in with girls her own age. I'd like you to help make her feel welcome."

"I don't think I can do that."

"Why not?"

"She's destroyed Travis's reputation. People say the most awful things about him now. And he's lost all his friends because of her."

"Sara's a member of the Church. She needs to know we love her."

"That's just it, I don't love her. Ask somebody else to do it."

"You're the one God wants to help Sara. I've prayed about this. Don't you think you ought to pray about it too?"

Kathy promised she would pray.

But she didn't.


SARA RETURNED TO SCHOOL the Monday after the trial ended. Joan and Travis accompanied her to the principal's office, and Joan met privately with the guidance counselor to explain Sara's situation. Travis sat with Sara and helped her work out a schedule of classes. It wasn't an easy task, considering she was arriving in the middle of a school year. Sara didn't much care what she took so long as she was in school again.

Outside the office, a throng of students passed by.

A minute later Joan returned with the guidance counselor. Together they worked out a schedule of classes for her. Then it was time for Joan to leave. She turned to Travis. "Take care of my girl."

"I will."

"Good. Well, I'd better go." She gave Sara a hug, then left.

"First we need to find your locker," Travis said.

Sara showed him the card with the locker number and combination. He led her down the hall amidst a sea of students. As they proceeded, he noticed a couple of boys smirking at them. Once they found her locker, Travis showed her how to work the combination. The class bell rang.

"I'm scared," she said.

"Don't worry. It'll be all right. I'll walk you to each class, and we'll have lunch together."

"Do I look okay?"

"You look great. Where's your first class?"

She looked at her schedule. "Room 203."

"I'll take you there."

When they reached room 203, she hesitated.

"It's going to be okay," he said. "I'll be here waiting for you as soon as class is over."

She nodded. "Well, I guess I'd better go. See you later." She entered the room. The teacher stopped her lecture and asked what Sara wanted. Sara said she was a new student. Travis stood outside, watching the others stare at Sara. For most, there was only mild curiosity. But with one or two, Travis could tell they'd heard stories about her.

For lunch Travis and Sara ate together. Nobody else came to join them. "They're talking about us, aren't they," she said.

"I don't know. Maybe so."

After lunch, they left the cafeteria and started back toward Sara's locker. As they passed a group of boys, someone called Sara a dirty name.

Travis stopped and walked back to them. He was ready to fight them all. "Who said that?"

"Said what?"

"You know what it was."

"I didn't hear anything. Did you guys hear anything?"

"I didn't hear anything."

Sara came to him. "Travis, never mind. Let's go."

Travis protectively reached out and held her hand, and they continued on their way. "I'll take you home now if you want me to," he said.

"I'm staying. Travis, I really think it'd be better if you'd let me do this myself."

"Why?"

"Because those guys just love baiting you. It'll be better if I just deal with it myself. I'll meet you after school, okay?"

After school he met Sara at her locker. As they walked into the parking lot, a car full of boys sped by. One of them unrolled his window and yelled an obscenity at Sara.

"I'm sorry," Travis said.

Travis had permission to use his mother's car because it was Sara's first week of school. "Don't tell Joan anything about what's happening in school," she said as he pulled up in front of her house.

"Why not?"

"I don't want her to worry about me. I can handle it. The talk will die out after a while."

Travis went home. He tried to study, but it was no use. After supper he went over to see Sara. As they watched TV, he put his arm around her. He wanted to protect her from ever being hurt again.

They watched TV for a couple of hours and then his mother called to tell him it was time to come home.

When he walked in the house, his parents were waiting. "How did things go for Sara at school today?" his mother asked.

"All right." He had decided not to tell them anything.

"Travis, we love you. We'd do anything to help you," his father said.

"If you're hurting, please tell us," his mother added.

Suddenly it was like when he was little and got hurt. He'd run home with no tears, trying to be a brave boy, but the minute he stepped in the door and saw his mother, the tears would come and she would hold him and make it all better. That was how he felt now. "They made fun of her," he whispered, barely able to keep from losing control.

"Is there anything we can do?" his father asked.

"No."

"Yes there is, Travis," his mother said.

"What?"

"We can pray."

They knelt down and had family prayer.


WHEN KATHY CAME HOME from the library that night, she also was troubled. "Mom, I need to talk to you."

"What's wrong?"

"There's so much pressure on me lately. I think I'm getting an ulcer."

"Are you having trouble with your classes?"

"It's not that. Sara's in school now, and people say such ugly things about her. Everyone knows she got pregnant and had a kid. So why does Travis hold hands with her and walk her to class? People make fun of them all the time. It's all Sara's fault. I hate her. I know I shouldn't, but I do, and when people say bad things about her, a part of me is glad they're saying it."

"Kathy, you need to be Sara's friend."

"I can't do that."

"Why not?"

"I just can't. Mom, if you only knew what they're saying about her. If I spend time with her, they might think I'm like that too."

"Are the things they say about her true?"

"No."

"Well then? She needs you, Kathy. Be her friend."

"You sound just like the bishop. He asked me to do that too. Look, I'm sorry I even came to you. I'll work this out myself, okay? I'm going to bed now."

"Before you leave, just let me read one passage of scripture to you."

"No, Mom, I feel bad enough without you preaching to me."

Her mother turned to a page in the Book of Mormon. "This is what members of the Church are supposed to do for each other: '. . . and are willing to bear one another's burdens, that they may be light; yea, and are willing to mourn with those that mourn; yea, and comfort those that stand in need of comfort.'"

Kathy turned and ran to her room.


TRAVIS COULDN'T SLEEP that night. At one o'clock he got up and tried to do some homework, but it was useless because he couldn't concentrate. He kept worrying about what would happen the next day in school.

At one thirty he made a phone call. It rang a long time and then Alan's mother sleepily answered it. "Hello."

"Is Alan there?"

"Alan's asleep. Do you know what time it is? Who is this?"

"I've got to talk to Alan. Please get him."

"This is Travis, isn't it?"

"Yes."

"I thought so. What sort of trouble have you gotten yourself into this time?"

"Let me talk to Alan."

"Alan needs his sleep."

"Please, it's very important."

"Give me the message, and then I'll tell him in the morning."

Travis could see that he wasn't going to get through to Alan. "Tell him to quit telling lies about Sara."

"Alan doesn't tell lies."

"He's made up things about Sara."

"What sort of things?"

He told her. She was very offended at what he said and was certain Travis was making the whole thing up. She hung up on him.

Travis went to the TV room and played a video game until three thirty. Then he fell asleep on the couch.

# Chapter Seventeen

THE NEXT MORNING, after walking Sara to class, Travis entered the boys' rest room on the first floor. Scrawled on the wall was a handwritten message, "For a good time, call Sara Corwin." Included was Sara's phone number.

Travis was stunned that anyone could be so cruel. He rummaged in his book bag for an eraser, and in a minute the message was gone. He staggered into the hall and stared at the students streaming by, wondering who'd written the message. There was no way to know.

He found the message in the rest room on the second floor too. He attacked it with an eraser until it was gone. The bell rang and he decided against going to class. He had to rid the school of any more signs like that. What if someone believed the message and phoned Sara?

He found similar messages in the rest room as well as above the drinking fountain on the third floor. All of the writing looked as if it had been written by the same person. And in the boys' locker room he found a distorted cartoon figure of a woman sketched on the wall with Sara's name and phone number written under it.

When first period ended, he walked Sara to her next class. There were no signs along their route, but after he left her, he found one tacked on a bulletin board.

He skipped class all morning. Instead he wandered up and down the halls, looking for messages. After each class change, a new crop appeared. He realized that someone was enjoying tormenting them.

He and Sara had agreed to meet each other at her
locker at noon and then go to lunch. At eleven o'clock,
not finding any more messages, he went to the library
and rested his head on the table. He wished the day was
over.

Ten minutes before noon, he decided to go to Sara's
locker in case she got out early. As he turned a corner, he
saw her locker. He gasped. Someone had painted a dirty
word on it in bright red paint. The word was meant to be
read from top to bottom, and the letters ran the length of
the locker. It was much too big to get rid of with an
eraser. Travis pulled off his sweater and started rubbing
the first letter of the word.

By the time the class bell rang, he'd managed to re-
move the first letter of the word. Students, more curious
than malicious, stopped to watch. Travis turned around.
"Please, somebody, help me."

Two boys and a girl stepped out of the crowd. "What
can we use to get this off?" the girl asked.

"Go to the rest room and get some paper towels.
Hurry up. We've got to get it off before Sara comes."

The girl hurried off to get some paper towels.

Travis saw Sara coming down the hall toward him.
He turned and rubbed as hard as he could on her locker.
Maybe he could get enough of it off so she wouldn't be
able to tell what it was.


KATHY WAS ONE OF THOSE in the hallway who'd
stopped to see Travis rubbing the word off Sara's locker.
Even though the first letter was gone, she could tell what
the word was. It was a horrible insult for any girl to be
called that. "This has gone too far," Kathy said to a girl
standing next to her.

"Well, from what I hear, she deserves it."

"The stories about her aren't true. Somebody should say something to make people stop hurting her."

"If that's the way you feel, why don't you?"

Kathy wavered. Before she could decide, she looked down the hall and saw Sara coming.


SARA WALKED THROUGH THE CROWD and saw Travis frantically wiping his sweater across the word. Sara knew what the word was. She'd been called it several times in the last two days.

Travis turned to face her. "I'm sorry. I tried. I didn't want you to have to see it." He seemed beaten and confused. She asked him to take her to lunch, but he said he didn't want to leave until the word was completely gone from her locker. "It doesn't matter," she said. She gently led him through the crowd toward the cafeteria.

As they stood in the cafeteria line, he knew people were talking about the word on Sara's locker. They got their food and headed for a corner table. On his way there, he saw Kathy in line. He stopped and stared at her. "Why won't you help us?" She looked down and wouldn't say anything. He shook his head and went to join Sara. They tried to eat, but they weren't very hungry.


AFTER LUNCH they walked to the building next door for seminary. Travis had been looking forward to it all day. Maybe people wouldn't be very friendly to them, but at least they'd be left alone.

During the lesson, a girl in front of them turned and handed Sara a note addressed to her. It was folded in half. Sara read it, then quickly slipped it into a book.

"What did it say?" Travis whispered.

She wouldn't tell him.

"Let me see it."

"No."

He grabbed her book and retrieved the note. It read, "We don't need your kind here."

Travis stood up, his face contorted with disappointment and anger. The teacher stopped talking. The room grew silent. "How can you be so cruel? Sara never hurt any of you. I'm so ashamed of you all." He let the note fall to the floor. "C'mon, Sara, we don't belong here."

They put on their coats and went outside. It was beginning to snow.

As the door closed behind them, the class remained silent. *Somebody ought to do something,* Kathy thought.

The seminary teacher picked up the note and read it to himself, then looked at the students. "Who wrote this?"

Nobody said anything. He opened his Bible and read: "'By this shall all men know that ye are my disciples, if ye have love one to another.'" He slammed the book shut with a dull, angry thud. "I can't see any point in going on with a lesson, can you? The time's yours to use as you see fit." He put on his coat and then rushed out to try and catch up with Travis and Sara.

Kathy knew what she must do now, what God had wanted her to do all along. She walked to the front of the class. "I need to tell you the truth about Sara Corwin . . ."

IN THE PARKING LOT, Travis and Sara got in the car. "You see how they are?" he said. "We can't stay here. We've got to move away to where nobody'll ever hurt you again. Let's get married and move to California."

Sara couldn't seem to think very clearly. She knew Travis would always be good to her. Maybe getting married to him would be the thing to do.

As they turned onto the street, Sara glanced over and saw their seminary teacher in the parking lot looking for them. She told Travis. "I don't care anymore," he said.

They drove to the courthouse. "We want to get married," Travis told the clerk at the marriage license office.

"Fill this out," she said, handing them a form and then returning to her desk. Travis began to fill out the application.

"What about your mission?" Sara asked quietly.

"I'm not going."

"But you believe the Church is true, don't you?"

"What difference does that make if people in the Church treat each other so rotten?"

"But we're not even out of high school. We don't have any money."

"I'll get a job. The important thing is we'll be together, and nobody'll ever hurt you again. This is for the best. Trust me."

"I do, but I'm still not sure this is the right thing to do."

He touched her face. "You know I love you, don't you?"

"Yes, I know that."

"All right then."

They gave the completed application to the clerk. She frowned. "You're both just sixteen?" she asked.

"Yes."

"You'll need to get your parents' permission first."

Travis wasn't going to let anything stop him. "All right, we'll get permission and come back tomorrow."

They drove around town and listened to the radio. Sara leaned her head on his shoulder. He told her how nice California was. After a while they went to a drive-in and had hot chocolate. Then he drove her home. "I've never told you this before, but one time I wrote a song just for you," he said.

"Can I hear it?"

"Sure. After supper I'll play it for you, and then we'll ask permission to get married. Okay?"

"Travis . . ."

"Okay?"

She wasn't sure she wanted to get married but she didn't want to hurt his feelings. "Okay," she said reluctantly.

He smiled and squeezed her hand.

She sighed. It was so hard to know what to do.

AFTER SUPPER Sara came over. He had her sit next to him at the piano while he played the song he'd written for her. When it was over, she told him she loved it.

Since afternoon, they both had had second thoughts about getting married so soon. Travis realized he'd miss out on his chance to serve a mission. Not only that, he might never have a chance to finish college.

For her part Sara realized she wasn't ready for marriage, but she also knew how awful it was to walk down the halls at school and have people call her names. She wasn't sure how long she could stand being treated that way.

They both lingered at the piano, uncertain of what the night would bring.

The doorbell rang. Travis's mother answered it.

It was Kathy. "Joan says that Sara is here. Can I talk to her?"

"Yes, of course."

Kathy came in and saw Sara and Travis sitting together at the piano. "I'm sorry if I'm interrupting anything."

"It's all right."

This was the hardest thing Kathy'd ever done, but

she knew she had to do it. "Sara, I'm having a slumber party Friday night. I was wondering if you'd come to it. There'll be just some of the girls from school. We'll listen to music and eat chips and drink diet soda, and play some games, and," she smiled, "basically drive my parents crazy." She paused. "Actually, the truth is, the party's for you."

"Oh?"

"After you and Travis left seminary today, I told the class what you've been through. They asked me to come here and apologize. From now on, it won't be just you and Travis against the whole school. Everybody's going to help. A bunch of us girls want you to eat lunch with us every day." She smiled. "I guess Travis can eat with us too, if he can stand listening to girl-talk. The thing is, we want you to know we're sorry. All of us know better, but sometimes we forget. On Friday night Travis can show you where I live, but you can't stay, Travis, because my parents said no boys. Well, I'd better be going now."

Sara stood up. "Thank you. I'll be to your party."

"Great. Well, I have to go study. 'Bye."

Travis went outside with Kathy. He could hardly speak. "Thanks."

"Travis, don't worry anymore, okay? We've all decided that Sara'll never be alone in school or church again."

And in truth she wasn't.

# *Chapter Eighteen*

A FEW MONTHS LATER, Sara tossed and turned well into the night. Finally she got up and turned on the light, sat down at her desk, pulled out a sheet of paper, and began to write.

> *Dear Travis,*
> *I will always*

She crumpled that up, tossed it into the wastepaper basket, and began again.

> *Dearest Travis,*
> *I will never forget how much you've done for me.*

She tossed that away too.

Joan, wearing a robe, opened the door a crack. "Hon, are you okay?"

"I couldn't sleep, that's all."

"Is it anything you want to talk about?"

Sara sighed. "Yes, I guess so. It's about Travis."

Joan came in and sat on the bed. "What about him?"

"Even though I have other friends now, he still wants it to be just him and me. And if I even talk to another guy, he gets jealous. He keeps talking about us getting married after his mission. Suddenly it's like my whole life is set in concrete. Well, I'm not ready for that." She paused. "This is awful to say, but lately I've had that same trapped feeling I had with Dillon, that no matter what I do I can't escape." She stopped. "Are you mad at me?"

"No, why should I be?"

"Because I know you'd like it if Travis and I got married someday."

"Sara, all I want is for you to be happy. With or without Travis."

"It's not that I don't like Travis. He's still the greatest guy I've ever known. It's just that I want to see how I can get along by myself." She pointed to the wastebasket. "That's what I was doing, trying to write him a letter so he'd know how I feel. I'm not sure I can do it though. He's the best friend I've ever had. He stuck by me when things were tough. How can I tell him I want to break up?"

"Well, if it's any consolation, he already knows something's wrong. The other day he asked me what was wrong with you. He said he can see the old sadness in your eyes again."

"He always knows when I'm feeling bad. He's such a great guy. I must be crazy for wanting to break up, but I've got to do it. I mean, for the first time in my life, I feel good about myself. I can't spend my life leaning on him. I've got to be free for a while. Does that make sense?"

"Sure it does."

"Then help me write a letter to Travis explaining how I feel."

"Sara, he deserves to hear it from you personally."


SARA ASKED TRAVIS to take her on a hike to where they'd gone their first time together. It was Joan's idea for Sara to talk to Travis on a hike, where Sara would have time to explain how she felt.

As they parked the car and started up the trail, Sara and Travis were both strangely quiet. Sometimes Sara, knowing what was at the end of their climb, reached out for his hand and they'd walk side by side until the trail got too narrow and they had to walk single file again.

On top of the mountain, she laid out the food on a large flat boulder that would serve as a table. She had brought a white linen tablecloth and napkins and glass goblets. For lunch they had seedless grapes and two kinds of sliced cheese, hard rolls, and grape juice. He offered to help but she wanted to do it all herself.

They were both strangely subdued.

"I'll never forget what you said the first time we came here," she said while they ate.

"What was that?"

"You said, 'When you get on top you can see tomorrow coming.'"

"I remember. I remember everything that happened to us."

She sighed. This was not going to be easy.

"There's something you want to tell me, isn't there," he said.

"Yes."

"What is it?"

"I think we both need time to see other people and to develop our own interests."

"You do?"

"Yes. Joan and I had a long talk last night. It's for the best, Travis. It really is."

Travis felt betrayed. "I thought you cared about me."

"I do. I love you. You've done so much for me, but we're still so young, and I just think this'll be best for both of us. We've been getting serious too fast. But we'll still be friends. We'll always be friends. I just need some breathing room to find out who I really am."

Travis knew what was happening, but there didn't seem to be anything he could do to stop it.

She continued. "I know some girls will go with a guy all through high school and college and then end up marrying him, but I can't do that. I'm still getting over what Dillon did to me. There're still so many things I have to work out in my mind." As long as she looked at the valley below, she was all right. But then she looked over at Travis and broke down.

Travis watched her cry. He was sorry she was sad, but this time she'd have to face it alone. "We'd better start back," he said quietly. "It looks like rain."

# Chapter Nineteen

FOUR YEARS LATER Travis returned from his mission. In that time much had happened. Sara had been officially adopted by Joan and Gary. She'd worked her way through two years of college at USU. Since they'd remained good friends, she'd written to him faithfully every week. He began to have hopes that things would work out for them after he returned home.

During his eighteenth month in the mission field, she wrote and told him about meeting a returned missionary in her campus ward. His name was Loren.

During his twenty-second month, she wrote and told him that Loren had asked her to marry him, and that she had accepted.

During his twenty-third month, she sent him a wedding invitation, along with a brief note thanking him for all he'd done for her.

The wedding was scheduled for Friday, one day after he arrived home from his mission.

TRAVIS STOOD in the reception line as it slowly inched its way toward the wedding party. Finally he stood in front of Joan. He went to shake her hand, but that wasn't good enough for her. "Travis, this is great! I finally have a good reason to hug you."

It must have been contagious, because Gary hugged him too.

And then he stood in front of Sara. He had planned just to shake her hand, but Joan was having too good a time being Mother of the Bride. "Travis," she teased, "you are going to kiss the bride, aren't you? This is your last chance, so you'd better take advantage of it."

He blushed. "Joan, give me a break. I just got back from a mission."

"Sara, I think it's up to you," Joan teased.

"My pleasure," Sara said. She kissed him on the cheek, then turned to her husband. "Loren, this is Travis. He's the one I told you about, the one who singlehandedly got me through high school."

They shook hands. Loren was a likable enough man. "Sara's told me all about you. Thanks for being her friend when she needed it most."

"Sure. Congratulations. You've got yourself a wonderful bride."

"I know that."

Next he met Loren's parents. They were from Apple Valley, California. He asked them how the apples were doing, and they laughed and said the whole place was a desert and that they'd been there ten years and were still trying to catch the person who'd called it Apple Valley.

At the refreshment table, he picked up a piece of wedding cake and a glass of punch, then went to sit with his parents, who'd come earlier.

"She's a beautiful bride, isn't she," his mother said.

"Yes, very."

"And she seems so confident and at peace with herself."

A few minutes later his parents left. Alan, who'd been home from his mission for two months, came over and sat down next to him. "I'm glad things turned out well for Sara," he said. He cleared his throat. "Travis, I have a confession to make. I was the one who wrote those things about Sara in the rest rooms. And before that, I made up stories about her. I just wanted you to know how bad I feel about it now. I've told Sara about it. She says she forgives me. She says she's forgiven everyone."

A few minutes later Travis got up to leave. He made it as far as the hallway before he heard a voice call out his name. He turned around. A vaguely familiar, attractive young woman was coming toward him. "My parents said you were back from your mission," she said. "How are you? I'm attending the university, but I just had to come here for Sara's wedding."

"Kathy?"

"Yes, that's me."

"You look great! What have you done to yourself?"

She laughed. "You make it sound like a major salvage job, you know, like raising the *Titanic* from the ocean."

He blushed. "No, not really, I didn't mean that. It's just that . . . in high school, you weren't . . . well, you were okay, of course, but now . . . I mean, now you're different . . . special . . ."

She burst out laughing. "Oh great! He thinks I'm special."

Travis panicked. Why was she laughing? He realized he didn't know what to say to a girl anymore. "Would you like to hear about my mission?" he blurted out.

She was enjoying watching him squirm. "The old mission ploy, hey? What's the matter, Travis, a little rusty?"

"Of course. Yesterday I was Elder Fitzgerald. Today I don't know who I am."

"Hey, it's okay. I'll fill in until you get the hang of it again. Just tell me what you want, and I'll tell you what to say to get it."

He glanced back. Looking at Sara for the last time

made him feel as if a part of him had died. He turned to Kathy. "I guess I need someone to talk with."

"Anyone in particular?"

"You."

"Okay, ask me out for a dish of ice cream."

"Would you like to go out for a dish of ice cream?"

"Yes. There, that wasn't too hard, was it?"

They went to a restaurant, where they made mostly small talk. Then they got in his car and drove around. By this time it was dark and they couldn't see each other's face. It seemed a good time for true confessions. "Is it hard for you to see Sara married to someone else?" Kathy asked.

"Yes, very."

"But at least you know you helped her get to where she is today. There must be some satisfaction in that. Travis, why didn't it work out between you two?"

"She had to move away from me to prove she'd gotten over what happened to her."

"Travis, I loved her too, you know. We became so close."

"I'm not sure I'll ever be able to forget her."

"Don't even try. She was an important part of your growing up." She paused. "Sometime, though, you'll need to move on with your life."

A few minutes later he walked her to her door.

"How long will you be in town?" he asked.

"Just until Sunday night. Then I have to get back for classes."

"You probably have a million guys chasing you at school."

"A few." She paused, not knowing if she should tell him or not. "But you know what? I've never met anybody like you. I guess I've never told you before, but you're my number one hero from our high school days—because of how you stood by Sara when she needed you."

He'd been out of circulation for two years, but it seemed like she was encouraging him. "Kathy, would you like to go on a hike with me in the morning?"

She smiled. "I'd like that very much."

They arranged the time and then he said good night and left.

He went home. His mom and dad were waiting up so they could have family prayer with him. As he knelt beside them, he realized how the pattern his parents had set, like family prayer, had seen them all through the tough times.

His dad offered the prayer. Afterwards, they stayed up and talked for a long time.

It was good to be home again.